DOUBLE E I

Slick Rock 2

Becca Van

MENAGE EVERLASTING

Siren Publishing, Inc.
www.SirenPublishing.com

A SIREN PUBLISHING BOOK
IMPRINT: Ménage Everlasting

DOUBLE E RANCH
Copyright © 2012 by Becca Van

ISBN-10: 1-61926-618-0
ISBN-13: 978-1-61926-618-6

First Printing: January 2012

Cover design by Les Byerley
All art and logo copyright © 2012 by Siren Publishing, Inc.

Printed in the U.S.A.

PUBLISHER
Siren Publishing, Inc.
www.SirenPublishing.com

DEDICATION

I would like to dedicate this book to all the staff at Siren-BookStrand for their hard work.

A special thanks to Diana and Kristen.

DOUBLE E RANCH

Slick Rock 2

BECCA VAN
Copyright © 2012

Chapter One

Felicity Wagner pulled up next to the long, large ranch house, ten miles outside of Slick Rock, Colorado, turned off the ignition to her small car, took a deep breath, and got out. She walked up the steps to the wide veranda running the length of the house, raised her fist, and knocked on the door. She was hoping she wouldn't have to turn around and find somewhere to stay the night. She was down to her last three hundred dollars and was desperately hoping she would land this job. She waited nervously, shifting from foot to foot, hoping someone would answer the door soon. She turned her head away from the door and looked around at the corral, barns, and other sheds she could see not more than fifty yards away from the house. As she looked, she raised her hand to knock again. Felicity gasped as her fist landed on something other than the door, making her turn back quickly. She felt her cheeks flush as she saw the tall, brawny man standing in the open doorway with a grin on his face.

"Sorry," Felicity said as she lowered her eyes to her feet. The first look she got of the man made tingles of warmth shoot up and down her spine, and then the warmth spread to her chest and lower down in her belly.

"No problem," the man replied in a deep, sexy drawl. "How can I help you?"

"I wanted to apply for the ranch hand job you had advertised in the local paper. Has the position been filled yet?"

"No. What's your name, darlin'?"

"Oh, sorry. Felicity Wagner. Pleased to meet you Mister…"

"Billy Eagle. Why don't you come on inside and answer a few questions for me, Felicity," Billy stated, moving back and allowing Felicity into his house.

Felicity followed Billy into the kitchen where she saw another man with similar features sitting at the kitchen table, drinking from a mug. Felicity hesitated, not wanting to be presumptuous and take a seat without being asked.

"Have a seat, Felicity. Can I get you some coffee?" Billy asked. Felicity accepted the coffee but declined his offer of cream and sugar since she took her coffee black. She was feeling rather uncomfortable because since she had followed Billy into the kitchen, the other man hadn't taken his eyes off of her.

"Felicity, this is my brother, Tom. Tom, Felicity. She's here about the ranch hand position," Billy explained.

Felicity watched as Tom sized her up. His eyes perused her from head to toe. She felt her cheeks burning again as she watched Tom lean back in his chair, fold his arms across his massive chest, and stare at her some more.

"Is that right? How old are you, Felicity?" Tom asked in a deep, gravelly voice.

Felicity had to bite the inside of her cheek to prevent the shiver working its way up and down her spine from making itself noticeable to the two men as Tom's voice flowed over her.

"I'm twenty-two, Mister Eagle. What has my age got to do with anything?" Felicity asked belligerently.

"Just wanting to make sure you're old enough. You don't look a day over fifteen. My name is Tom, not Mister Eagle," Tom stated with a smirk.

"Okay, Tom. I can't help the way I look. I thought as long as I can do my job nothing else should matter."

* * * *

"What makes you think you can do the work of a man, little girl?" Tom goaded, trying to hide his grin. He couldn't believe how easy it was to rile the gorgeous, petite woman sitting across from him. He knew she wanted to be giving him a dressing down but was trying to hold back so she wouldn't jeopardize her chances of getting the job. He was having a lot of fun, and he knew Billy was also trying to hide his amusement. Tom looked over and saw Billy looking at him, and he knew the gleam in his brother's eyes would have been obvious to anyone who knew him.

Neither he nor his brother could take his eyes off the little woman. She was so small compared to him. He and his brother both stood quite a bit over six feet, and the woman sitting in their kitchen glaring at him couldn't have been more than five two. Her hair was as black as midnight. She had it pulled back from her face with a rubber band, and it looked to be in a loop of sorts, as well. He was itching to pull her hair free and see how long it was. Her eyes were blue, but when she was riled they seemed to turn to a deep violet color. He knew he could lose himself in those eyes. She was wearing denim blue jeans and a flannel shirt, of which the first three buttons were undone. He could just make out a hint of cleavage, which was enough to tempt any saint. She had curves in all the right places as far as he could see, but for some reason she didn't tuck her shirt in. It looked like she was trying to hide her curves from prying eyes. He wondered if she was one of those women who thought she could do anything a man could. One of those modern women who were into portraying themselves as a feminist suffragette.

Tom and Billy were fine with women who wanted to be like men, as long as it wasn't around them. They had both been searching for a woman who would be independent and not a clinging vine, but also feminine enough to hand over all her control to them. They wanted a submissive woman to share between them, especially in the bedroom. Tom couldn't believe how smooth and creamy her skin looked. She looked to be so soft and gentle, yet the fire in her eyes said otherwise. If she was a ranch hand, how the hell had she kept her skin so white and soft?

* * * *

"I grew up on a ranch. I can ride, shoot, and round up as good as any man. If you don't believe me, why not put me to a test? If you like what I can do, then maybe I can work for you," Felicity spat out through clenched teeth. God, what had she gotten herself into?

The two men eying her from across the table were two of the sexiest, handsomest men she'd ever set eyes on. Their skin was a sexy bronzed color, showing their Indian heritage. They both had shoulder-length black hair and brown eyes. They were both well over six feet in height, making her feel like a small child. They had sharp cheekbones and square, chiseled jaws. Their bodies were a testament to all the hard physical work she knew they did on their ranch, but Tom was a lot broader and more muscular than Billy. He reminded her of a large tree trunk. His hands looked too big to be holding on to the coffee mug he was sipping on. It was a wonder it hadn't broken apart in his hands. She wondered if he was sexist against women doing men's work and, if so, why he felt a woman wasn't as good as a man.

"Now, that's not such a bad idea, Tom. Why not let this here little girl show us what she's made of?" Billy asked.

"All right, we have a bunch of calves to round up and get into the corral for branding. You can come with us and show us what you've got. I'll decide after I've seen you in action," Tom stated as he rubbed his whiskered jaw.

"Thank you, Mister Eagle."

"Tom and Billy," Tom replied.

"Tom."

Felicity watched as Tom pushed his chair back and stood up. He walked over to Felicity and pulled her chair out as she stood. She was so tiny she barely reached his chest. He kept his eyes on hers as she stepped back and waited for him to move first. She was a little intimidated by his size and wanted him to lead the way out of the house.

"Jack, can you tack up for us and get Zeus saddled up, as well?" Tom called out and then turned back to her. "Jack's the foreman of the Double E Ranch." Felicity saw Jack look to his boss and wondered why he looked so incredulous, but the foreman replied without question.

"Sure thing, boss," Jack replied.

"Tom, what—"

"Leave it, Billy," Tom commanded in a hard voice.

Felicity wondered what was going on, but didn't dare ask. Tom's hard, commanding voice gave her goose bumps. She had a feeling she was in over her head, but couldn't figure out why.

Felicity caught sight of Jack leading three horses out of the barn. They were all tacked up, just waiting to be mounted. The big black stallion prancing skittishly drew her eye. He was such a gorgeous animal. His muscles rippled as he moved, and his black coat was so dark she could see traces of blue in it. He had to stand at least seventeen hands, and she knew he would be a handful for anyone who rode him. She guessed he was probably Tom's horse. He would certainly need a large, muscular horse to ride. The other horses were just as large, but Zeus had more fire in him.

Felicity watched as Tom moved over to Zeus, grabbed his bridle, and led the horse toward her. Felicity didn't move, not wanting him to know he intimidated her, but she hoped like hell he was leading that horse to her. She would show that arrogant ass she wasn't some prissy little female.

"You get to ride Zeus here. Let me warn you though, he's a bit of a handful," Tom advised.

"Oh, good. I love a feisty horse," Felicity said with a grin.

"Okay, let's get going. I want to be finished before nightfall," Tom stated as he mounted.

Felicity watched as Billy mounted his horse. Then when she knew the two men were watching her to see how such a small woman would mount such a large horse, she hid her grin. She vaulted into the saddle without so much as using a stirrup. Zeus, obviously not used to be mounted in such a way, protested. He reared up and tried to throw her. Felicity clung to the horse's sides with her knees and legs, pulled on the bridle gently, all the while crooning to the finicky stallion. When she had the large animal under control, she looked over to the two men and had to bite her tongue to stop the laugh bubbling up from her chest. They looked to be in shock.

* * * *

Tom nudged his mount and set off at a hard gallop. Not once did he look back to see if Felicity was following or having trouble keeping up. He knew Billy would keep an eye on her and call out if there was trouble. Tom slowed the pace down after letting his mount run for about fifteen minutes. He didn't want to tire his horse out too much before they could round up all the calves. He saw movement in his peripheral vision and knew Felicity and Billy were riding just a little back from him to his right. So it seemed the little woman could ride even better than she'd said. He wondered who had taught her. She didn't seem to be having any trouble with Zeus at all.

Tom pulled to a stop on the top of a small hill. He breathed in the clean, fresh air as he watched the calves frolicking and grazing in the paddock below. There were at least fifty calves that needed to be brought into the corral. Usually he let his foreman Jack and the ranch hands deal with the roundup, but he really wanted to see what this little woman was made of. But more importantly he wanted her in his bed. He wondered if he could put his conceitedness aside for a change. He doubted it.

Tom knew most of the women in Slick Rock thought of him as a sexist, arrogant bastard. He didn't care though. He knew what he wanted in a woman, and he usually wasn't prepared to settle for anything else. But seeing Felicity made him wonder if he could change his way of thinking. Maybe he could let a woman be who she was and work the way she wanted throughout the day, as long as she became submissive in the bedroom. He rubbed his hand over his face and gave a sigh. It was definitely worth thinking about.

"We need to round up the calves down in that paddock and get them back to the corral near the house," Tom said to Felicity without looking at her. "Come on, let's get this done."

The three of them worked in tandem. It took them less than two hours to get the calves back into the corral. Tom couldn't believe how hard Felicity worked. She became one with her horse and took off like lightning when some of the calves broke free of the herd. She and Zeus worked like they had been together for years. She had Zeus cutting the cattle off before they could get too far away. In fact, if he had been asked to compare her skills to Jack, he would have had to say Felicity was much better, and that was saying something.

Jack had the branding iron nice and hot by the time the three of them had all the calves in the corral. The other four ranch hands were ready and waiting to help with the tedious, backbreaking job. Tom decided to test the mettle of the small woman helping them out for the afternoon, wondering if she'd baulk at the idea of burning a brand into the hide of the calves.

"Felicity, I want you to help Jack with the branding. The ranch hands can bring the calves to you and hold 'em down. I need to get some paperwork done. I'll be in my office, Jack. Billy, I need some help, come with me," Tom demanded as he led his mount to the barn.

After pulling the tack from their horses, giving their mounts a rubdown, and seeing their horses were watered and fed, Tom led the way back to the house. He could see Billy was itching to bitch at him for the way he had treated Felicity, but knew his brother would hold his tongue until they got back to the house, away from prying ears.

"What the fuck's gotten into you, Tom? Why the hell did you put that little girl on Zeus? You could have gotten her killed," Billy yelled.

"I wanted to see what she was made of. She sure showed me up, now didn't she?" Tom said with a grin.

"Yep, she sure did. She's better in the saddle than Jack. Don't you tell him I said that," Billy said with a smile. "She sure knows how to handle ranch work. So, what do you think?"

"Not sure. Gonna have to take a week or so to see. She's not very submissive. You saw the fire in her eyes when I was baiting her, as much as I did. She's a feisty little thing. But she's had me hard since the moment she walked into the kitchen."

"Yeah, me too. She's so sexy. I can't wait to strip her clothes off and get a good look at that body she's trying to hide," Billy stated.

"Those lips of hers are so full. They're just begging for a man to kiss." Tom groaned, closing his eyes as he imagined those lips wrapped around his cock. "We'll have to let her feel her way around here a bit before we put our moves on her. I don't want her running away."

"So are we in accordance on this?" Billy asked as he rubbed his hands together.

"Yeah, we are, little brother."

* * * *

Felicity hadn't had to brand cattle for a long time. So by the time they were finished, her back was aching from bending over, and her arms and legs were aching as well. She had a headache from all the noise and dust, and since she hadn't had a break since she first arrived on the Double E Ranch, she was thirsty and slightly dehydrated. She helped Jack brand the last calf, stood up, and stretched her tired, aching muscles. She heard voices off to the side of the corral and turned her head to see Tom and Billy heading their way.

"I see you've finished with the branding. I want you to come up to the house for a discussion," Tom stated as he drew up beside her, and then she saw him turn toward Jack.

"Thanks, Jack," Tom said, giving Jack a thumbs-up.

Felicity followed Tom and Billy into the house. They led her to a room off the end of a long hallway, and she knew she was in their office. There were two desks set up with laptops and phones on each timber surface. There were a couple of spare chairs off to the side of the room, as well as a small sofa. Felicity eyed the sofa with longing but turned her head away from it to face the two men leaning side by side on one of the desks, their arms crossed over their broad, muscular chests.

"Take a seat, Felicity," Billy commanded, indicating the sofa.

Felicity took him at his word and sank onto the cushion gratefully, hoping neither man could see how she was stiffening up already.

"We'd like to offer you the position of ranch hand. You've proved you're more than capable of doing the job. You'll be paid cash for today, as today is payday. You'll be paid weekly just like the rest of the hands. I want you living on this ranch, just like the other hands do, but since we don't have a separate bunkhouse for women, you'll be staying in this house. We have a spare room you can use. You'll get all meals supplied, as well as a roof over your head. We want you to sign a contract just like all the other hands have. The contract is for twelve months, but if we feel you have breached any of our rules, we can terminate your employment, effective immediately. You are not to date any of the ranch hands. We don't want relationships causing any trouble between the hands. So now the decision is yours. Do you want the job, Felicity?" Tom asked.

"Yes. Thank you. I do. There won't be any dating, I don't date. I don't think it's right that I live in your house, though. I don't want to be seen as given preferential treatment just because I'm female," Felicity asserted.

"I don't care what you want, little girl. There is no way in hell I'm putting you in the bunkhouse with those men. Think about the trouble having a woman amongst them would cause," Tom replied.

"Don't they have separate rooms?" Felicity asked.

"Yes, they do have their own rooms, but the shower is shared between them all. How would you like to have five big, horny men holding you down to have their way with you?" Tom almost spat out.

Felicity paled as the image of five men raping her coalesced in her mind. It looked like she was staying in their house and not the bunkhouse, after all. "Okay. I'll stay in your guest room. Thanks."

"I make the rules in this house and on this ranch. What I say goes. No arguing, you have to accept mine and Billy's word as law. Do you have a problem with that?"

"No. As long as your rules are fair and not discriminatory," Felicity replied.

"I don't care whether you think my rules are discriminatory or not. My rules are to be adhered to at all times. The rules I set in place are for everyone living and working on this ranch. They are to keep you and everyone else safe. Do you understand?" Tom rapped out.

"Yes."

"Will you obey my rules?"

"Yes," Felicity replied, her eyes on her feet.

"Okay. Here is your contract of employment. Read it over and then sign it. You can leave it on this desk. When you're done, come into the kitchen to find me. I'll show you to your room. If you give your car keys to Billy, he can unload your stuff and park your car in the carport," Tom stated then left the study.

Felicity stared after Tom, nibbling on her lower lip, wondering if she was doing the right thing. She had nowhere else to go. She didn't really have much of a choice. She picked up the pen on the desk and signed her name to the bottom of the contract. She looked up to see Billy standing in the doorway, eying her speculatively. She handed her car keys to Billy then headed toward the kitchen. She really needed a drink of water.

Chapter Two

Felicity sat down for lunch with the ranch hands. Over the last couple of weeks, Felicity had gotten into a routine of helping out in the stables, feeding the horses, and cleaning out stalls. She was actually relieved to be staying in the ranch house guest bedroom, and she knew it would have been uncomfortable if she was sharing the bunkhouse with five other men. Tom and Billy had been courteous but distant toward her, except at mealtimes. Everyone would convene in the large kitchen dining room where the elderly housekeeper, Nanette, would have the meals ready for serving, and share the food. The noise of seven men chatting at every meal could be quite loud and rambunctious.

Felicity was still trying to come to terms with the fact "the guest bedroom" was indeed the master bedroom of the house. She knew there was no way Tom would let her sleep in the bunkhouse. Not that she really wanted to. Felicity didn't participate much in the conversations at mealtimes. She was trying to keep a low profile. Even though she had always been more comfortable around men and she had a great rapport with Jack, the other ranch hands tended to keep to themselves. Except for James. Felicity had often caught James eying her like she was a mare in heat, and he was making her feel decidedly jumpy. Often James would "accidentally" bump into her, brush an arm against her breast, or nearly knock her over as he pretended not to see her. The man gave her the creeps. She hadn't said anything to Jack, Tom or Billy because she needed this job more than she needed her next breath of air. Plus, she didn't want to be seen as having led on any of the men on and therefore having caused trouble.

Felicity looked up from her plate of stew to find James once again leering at her body. She quickly lowered her head and tried to ignore the jerk. When lunch was done, Felicity was the first to head out and start on mucking out the stalls. She knew the men would linger over their coffee, as Tom and Billy always took the opportunity at mealtimes to catch up on things happening around the ranch.

Felicity had just moved Zeus out of his stall to the spare at the opposite end of the barn, preparing to begin mucking the stalls, when she heard footsteps heading in her direction. She raised her head to see James heading her way. She gave a mental groan then turned back to her task. She had just begun to rake out the stall when two bands of steel wrapped around her waist, hauling her back against a tall, rangy, masculine body. Felicity didn't need to turn her head to know it was James behind her. She stomped down on his toes as hard as she could, making him yelp with pain as he backed away from her.

"You think you're so high and mighty, don't ya, you little bitch? You think I don't see the way you're twitching your ass around all of us. You think you're way too good to live with all the other ranch hands. Well, you're nothing but a piece of ass, and I intend to have me some of that ass," James spat out. He lunged for Felicity, catching her arms as she swung the rake toward him. He caught it and pulled it from her hands before she could do any harm. He pushed her into Zeus's empty stall using all his strength, not caring if he hurt her or not. He had her up against the barn wall with her hands held above her head before she could blink.

"Let me go, you son of a bitch," Felicity ground out through clenched teeth.

"Now why would I want to do that?" James replied with a leer. He ground his hard cock against her stomach, making her feel physically ill.

Felicity struggled with him, knowing her actions were futile, but she wasn't going to let this asshole win. She tried to knee him in the groin, but because he was keeping her pinned with his body, she didn't quite reach her goal.

"Let me go, now, you bastard."

James didn't relent. He slammed his mouth down on hers, trying to push his tongue into her mouth. Felicity felt bile rise up from her stomach. She knew she was in big trouble. She didn't try fighting him, knowing it was useless. She held still and hoped he would get bored with her nonresponse. When he grabbed her hair and pulled hard, Felicity couldn't help her cry of pain. He used that involuntary act against her, immediately shoving his slimy tongue into her mouth. Felicity didn't hesitate. She bit down on his tongue hard. James pulled away from her with a yelp then backhanded her so hard across the face, she stumbled into the side wall of the stall, hitting her head. She slumped to the ground, both of her ears ringing as she saw stars in front of her eyes. She breathed deeply, trying to keep her wits about her, not wanting to give James the advantage by passing out.

Felicity felt rough hands tearing at her shirt, then cool air as her upper body was exposed. She opened her eyes to see James licking his lips as he stared at her chest. Felicity used her leg and kicked out at him with everything she had. She caught him on the thigh, not doing much damage, except to make him curse. She didn't see the fist coming her way, but felt the agony as it connected with her jaw. Pain exploded in her face and head, and then she slipped into a hurt-free world.

* * * *

Jack had just entered the barn to give Felicity some help cleaning out the stalls when he heard James curse. He looked down to the other end of the barn, but couldn't see him or Felicity. He knew that bastard was up to no good. He ran to the other end to see James's fist connect with Felicity's jaw. She was out cold on the ground, her shirt ripped open with bruises forming on her face and breasts. He gave a roar of fury. He hauled James away from Felicity by the back of his shirt, spun the other man around, and planted his fist into his face. The bastard didn't get up. Jack had broken the fucker's nose and knocked him out with one punch. Jack kicked James out of his way and knelt at Felicity's side. He pulled her ripped shirt over her chest, gently picked her small body up from the ground into his arms, and then ran for the ranch house, being careful not to jar the small woman he held. As he reached the ranch house veranda, he yelled for Tom and Billy.

Jack saw Tom flying out the door first, and he came to halt when he saw Jack and Felicity. Jack's employer opened it for him, and his boss stared down at the unconscious woman in his arms. Billy was on Tom's heels, and Jack could see the pain and fury in their faces.

"Who?" Billy snapped, and Jack saw him look at Felicity's face and ripped shirt.

"James. He's in the barn. I knocked him out," Jack replied.

The sound of Billy's yell of rage was enough to send chills down Jack's spine. Billy was out the door before he could say anything else.

"Bring her to the bedroom," Tom commanded through clenched teeth. Tom's voice was so full of fury, even Jack flinched as his boss led the way to Felicity's room.

Jack knew Tom watched as he gently laid Felicity on the bed and stepped back.

"Get Nanette to call for the doc," Tom ordered.

Jack left to do Tom's bidding.

* * * *

Tom could feel his hands shaking as he reached out to Felicity. He wanted to go and kill that bastard with his bare hands, but knew Felicity needed him more. He gently pulled her shirt from her body, hissing through his teeth when he saw her bruised breasts. He carefully worked the ripped shirt from her body, then her jeans, until Felicity was left in her bra and panties. He covered her with a blanket from the closet, headed to the bathroom for a wash cloth and warm water. Just as he was carefully washing Felicity's bruised, battered face, Nanette walked into the room. He heard her gasp of shock as she saw Felicity's face. She hurried over to Tom to help care for the small woman on the bed. Between the two of them, they had Felicity's face, arms, and chest washed, all dirt removed from her body. He knew Nanette was as concerned as he was because Felicity hadn't come around yet. The sound of the door slamming against the wall announced the arrival of Billy.

"Where is the bastard?" Tom asked his brother.

"He's gone. He must have come around when Jack was bringing her to the house. I was just in time to see the tail end of his car leaving the ranch. Fuck it. He got away, Tom."

"Once we have treated Felicity as much as we can, we'll let the doctor examine her and the sheriff take over. I don't think he'll ever show his face around here again. The bastard is a yellow-bellied coward," Tom replied as he stared down at Felicity.

The doctor arrived twenty minutes later. Even though he ordered Tom and Billy from the room, they wouldn't budge. They just both stood against the far wall, their arms crossed over their chests, glaring at the man. They watched Doc exam Felicity, trying to use his body to keep prying eyes away.

Tom listened as Doc muttered to himself as he worked. He saw the elderly man baulk, his voice becoming louder as examined Felicity.

"I can't believe someone could beat up such a small, helpless woman. She has bruises covering her cheeks, chest, and another beneath her jaw where a fist has connected with her skin. Her face is swollen, and she's suffering from a concussion. She should wake up pretty soon."

"If you need to get her to a hospital, then that's what we'll do," Tom bit out. He wanted her where he knew she was safe, so if she had to go to the hospital, he would organize guards for her. Otherwise he and Billy were going to be vigilant to the point of annoying but knew if Doc said Felicity needed to be hospitalized he would take her to the hospital himself.

Tom watched Doc as he froze on the spot when Felicity moaned. He and Doc watched her intently as she slowly opened her eyes, slammed her eyelids shut again, and clutched her head between her hands.

"Felicity, I'm Doctor Foster. How are you feeling?"

"Terrible," Felicity replied through dry, bruised lips.

"Now, I don't want you moving around too much. You have a bad concussion, which is no doubt making you feel sick. Your face is also swollen and bruised. You need to take it easy for at least a week. If the headache doesn't begin to go, you'll need to go to the hospital," Doc said.

"No insurance," Felicity replied.

"What's more important, money or your health? Can you open your eyes for me, little lady?" Doc asked.

Tom could see when Felicity opened her eyes that she was having trouble keeping them open. He could tell by the way she was blinking she couldn't see. He saw her flinch back away from Doc as he shone a light into her eyes.

"Sick," Felicity cried out as she slammed her eyelids shut again.

Tom knew Doc or he wouldn't have time to get a bucket for the ill woman. He saw Doc glance around the room, spy a trash can near the bedside table, grab it, help Felicity to roll to her side, and hold her head as she was ill. When she was done emptying her stomach, Doc looked over to him and Billy.

"Please bring a glass of water for the young lady," Doc demanded.

Tom sent Billy for the water, and his brother was back in moments with a glass in hand. He watched as Billy and Doc helped Felicity to take a drink and rinse her mouth. Then he saw Doc head to the bathroom, the sound of running water and the smell of disinfectant telling him Doc was cleaning the garbage can. Doc was back a few minutes later. Tom kept a watch over Felicity as she fell asleep. Doc turned to him and started giving instructions.

"I want you to keep an eye on this little girl for the next twenty-four to forty-eight hours. Wake her up every hour for the first twenty-four hours, make sure she knows where and who she is. After that you can wake her every four hours. If you have any concerns, or if her nausea and headache don't settle, call me right away. No pain medication at all until the headache has gone. You need to get some ice packs to bring down the bruising and swelling on her face."

"Thanks, Doc, I appreciate you coming out," Tom replied as he led Doc to the door.

"Billy, call the sheriff. I want him to look for that asshole and have him locked up for assault and attempted rape. Ask him to come out to the ranch so he can see what James did to Felicity," Tom commanded then walked back down the hall to keep an eye on their injured woman.

Tom greeted Sheriff Luke Sun-Walker with the familiarity of a long-standing friendship when he arrived at the Double E Ranch thirty minutes later. He led the sheriff into the kitchen and took a seat at the kitchen table after offering Luke a seat. Nanette handed him a cup of coffee as he, Billy, and Luke sat down to discuss what James had done to Felicity.

"You know I'm going to have to see her and take photos of her bruising. I know it's going to be hard for you, but it will be even harder for her. The last thing an attempted rape victim wants to do is relive their nightmare again. I'm real sorry to have to put her through that torture, but I need those photos for evidence. Nanette, can you come into the bedroom, too? Hopefully the presence of another female will help put Felicity at ease," Luke stated.

Tom led the way down the hallway to the bedroom, Billy, Nanette, and Luke following behind. Tom heard Luke suck in a breath as he saw Felicity's battered and bruised face. He was glad to see she looked like she was sleeping comfortably, and he didn't really want to disturb her, but knew it was best to get the business side of things over and done with. He knew Luke needed to question her so he could take down her statement. Tom watched as Nanette tried to wake Felicity as gently as she could. She stroked Felicity's forehead and called her name. Felicity didn't budge.

Tom was becoming concerned, so he walked to the bed, sat down on the side, placed his hand on Felicity's shoulder, and gently shook her, demanding, "Felicity, wake up."

Still, she didn't move or make any noise to indicate she had heard him. "Wake the fuck up, damn it," Tom bellowed, beyond worried for the small woman.

Tom sighed with relief when Felicity groaned at the sound of his voice.

* * * *

She didn't want to wake up. She knew if she did she would only feel pain. But the hand on her shoulder and the voice near her ear bellowing at her were so insistent she couldn't ignore them for long. She slowly opened her eyes, thankful the room was dim. Someone must have pulled the curtains over the window to keep the sunlight out. Her vision was blurry, but she could make out four people in the room. She recognized Nanette, Tom, and Billy but couldn't work out who else was there. In the end she was too tired to care. Her eyelids became too heavy to keep open, and they began to drift closed again.

"Felicity, don't you dare go back to sleep. Open your eyes, baby. Sheriff Luke Sun-Walker wants to ask you a few questions. He also needs to take some photos of your face and chest for evidence. Come on, baby, open those eyes," Tom demanded.

Felicity groaned again, lifted her arms, and cradled her aching head in her hands. She just wanted to be left alone and go back to sleep, but knew Tom wouldn't leave her alone until he had what he wanted. She opened her eyes once more, feeling sick to her stomach as everything moved unnaturally before her vision. A large man she'd never seen before was standing close to Tom's side.

"Felicity, this is Sheriff Luke Sun-Walker. He needs to ask you a few questions about James."

"Hi, Felicity," Luke said in a quiet, gentle voice as he knelt down on the floor beside her. "I know you're in pain, sweetheart, so I'll try not to keep you awake too long. Can you tell me what James did to you?"

"Water," Felicity croaked out from between her parched lips. She was grateful when Tom and Luke helped her to a half-sitting, half-reclining position against the pillows. Tom made sure her body was covered decently with the quilt, and Luke held the glass to her lips, letting Felicity sip a few times until she pushed the glass away.

Felicity continued to tell him all the details, up until she had hit her head. "He was standing over me, and I knew he was going to try and r–rape me, so I kicked him. He punched m–me. I don't remember what h–happened after th–that," Felicity finished on a sob.

"It's okay, baby. He can't hurt you anymore. He didn't get to you. Jack found him hurting you and knocked him out," Tom crooned in a soft voice as he smoothed a hand up and down her arm.

"I'm sorry I've had to upset you, Felicity, but I need to know more. Tom said Jack found you with your shirt ripped open. Did he hurt you, honey? Did he touch you where he shouldn't have?" asked Luke.

"I–I–I don't remember," Felicity sobbed out.

"Shh, it's okay now. That's okay. You may remember later. I need to take some photos of your face and chest, Felicity. Will you let me do that, so I can charge James when we find him?"

"You can't find him? Where is he?" Felicity asked, letting her fear show.

"It's all right. Don't you worry about a thing, sweetheart. I'll find him, and when I do, he'll be in jail for a long time. Will you let me take those photos, sweetheart?" Luke asked again.

Felicity clutched the sheet and blankets to her chest, curling herself into a small ball. "I…I can't."

"Shh, that's okay. What if I give the camera to Nanette and we let her take the photos? Can you deal with that?"

"Okay," Felicity agreed with a sniff, wiping a hand over her cheeks, wincing in pain as she touched her bruised face.

"Good girl. We'll leave the room and leave you in Nanette's capable hands. You just rest up and get better, all right? If you remember anything else, you let Nanette, Tom, or Billy know and they'll give me a call. Take care, sweetheart," Luke stated gently. Felicity watched as Tom and Billy left the room, Luke following after handing the digital camera over to Nanette.

* * * *

Luke looked up at Nanette when she handed the digital camera over to him without a word. She turned her back on him, trying to conceal her tears, but he had seen them and was worried about what he'd find on the camera.

Luke turned the camera on and knew the other two men could see his jaw clenching with anger the more he looked at the pictures. He wanted to find that bastard and kill him but, being the law, knew he would have to do everything by the book. Seeing Felicity, so small and fragile, with bruises marring her flesh had his whole body tense with anger. He looked up at Tom and Billy to see them eying him. He handed the digital camera over to Tom and Billy, not surprised when Billy slammed his fist down on the table. He wanted to do the same thing.

"We had Doc check her out. The bruising and swelling you saw. She's also got a concussion. Doc says we need to keep waking her every hour for the next twenty-four hours, then every four hours after that. She was sick when Doc was here, and he was thinking of putting her in the hospital," Tom stated.

"Son of a bitch," Luke hissed through clenched teeth. He eyed the two men and knew they had feelings for the little woman. He wanted to haul her out of here and take her to his place behind the sheriff's station. Luke knew she was the woman meant for him as soon as he had seen her beautiful, bruised face. He just wondered if the two men in front of him had any claim over her. Luke knew the two brothers shared women and were also dominant men who liked to be in control in the bedroom. Luke was also a dominant man, but had never thought about sharing a woman with anyone before. He tried to picture these two men pleasuring Felicity in front of him while he participated. He was surprised when he began to get hard.

"Are you two dating Felicity?" Luke asked as he took a sip of coffee from his mug.

"Not yet, but we're working on it. Why?" asked Tom.

"I want in," Luke replied, holding Tom's gaze with his own. There was no way in hell he was backing down. He wanted Felicity just as much, if not more, than the two men in front of him.

"Fuck it, Luke," Tom said as he wiped his hand down over his face. "I don't know how we are going to get that woman interested in one of us, let alone three, after what she's just been through. She's only been at the ranch a few weeks. We were trying to give her time to settle in before we made a move on her. I don't know what to do now that fucking asshole has abused her."

"I'm not going to back off. I'm not going to stand back and watch you two claim her. I want her just as much you do," Luke stated quietly, but firmly.

Luke turned his head as he heard Nanette stomping over to the large dining table. She made him jump as she slammed down a pot of coffee and glared at him and his two friends.

"I know I am only the cook and housekeeper, but I can't believe you three are talking this way about that little girl right now. She has only just been hurt. If I catch any of you putting the moves on that woman and scaring her, you will answer to me. Do you understand?"

"Yes, ma'am," Luke and his friends replied then grinned at each other when Nanette harrumphed and stomped away.

"I'd better get back to the office. I'll have an APB out on James within half an hour," Luke said as he rose to his feet. He was about to get into his truck when he turned back to Tom and Billy. "I'll be back for dinner. You'd better let Nanette know. I'll also be staying in the spare room from now on."

Luke saw Tom look at Billy, but his friend didn't reply as he got into his truck and drove away. He knew by the expression on his friends' faces they didn't really want to share Felicity with him, but his friends knew he wasn't about to back off.

Chapter Three

Felicity drifted in and out of sleep over the next twenty-four hours. Tom, Billy, and Sheriff Luke Sun-Walker took turns in waking her up throughout the night. The three men made sure she had a few sips of water every time they woke her up. She was getting mighty sick and tired of having them disturb her sleep, asking her stupid questions like what her name was, what day it was, et cetera.

Felicity finally woke up around lunchtime the next day, feeling tired, groggy, wrung out, and sore. Her face was hurting like a bitch, but at least her head wasn't throbbing as much anymore. Felicity climbed out of bed, took a shower, got dressed, and went to the kitchen looking for some coffee. She wasn't hungry, but coffee was definitely in the cards. She walked into the kitchen to see everyone crowded around the dining table, eating their lunch. She was surprised to see Sheriff Luke Sun-Walker sitting in the chair closest to the doorway, sharing a meal with her employers. She hadn't met the sheriff until she had been hurt, and now it seemed he was spending all his time with Tom and Billy. She had a hazy memory of Luke waking her up during the night, asking her questions, and giving her water to drink.

The chattering in the room stopped as all eyes turned toward her. Felicity felt her cheeks heat and lowered her eyes to the floor. She looked up again when she heard the scrape of a chair, and then she was being led to a spare seat beside the sheriff. Nanette bustled over, handed Felicity a mug of coffee, and placed an empty plate with utensils in front of her. She gave her a comforting pat on the shoulder before hurrying back over to the kitchen.

"How are you feeling, baby?" Tom asked from across the table.

"I'm fine," Felicity replied automatically.

"Well, you look like death warmed up. What are you doing out of bed? Doc said you had to take it easy," Billy asked from beside her.

"I'm fine, really," Felicity reiterated with a smile then winced as she felt pain pull at where her lip had been split.

"I think you should be back in bed, honey," Luke stated. He gently placed a finger beneath her chin and tilted her head toward him. She saw him studying her face and frowning as he looked at her. Felicity pulled her face away from the sheriff, lowered her eyes to the table as she picked up her mug of coffee. She tried to hide the wince of pain as the hot fluid connected with her split lip.

"Jack, I want to thank you for helping me. Tom told me what you did. So thanks," Felicity said as she looked at her foreman.

Jack didn't reply, just gave her a smile and shrug of his shoulders then looked away again.

Felicity felt like an intruder. Ever since she had walked into the dining room, the men had stopped talking, and they were all staring at her. She picked up her coffee, stood up, and headed to the back door.

Luke grabbed her wrist gently, stopping her progress, then asked her, "Where are you going? You haven't had anything to eat. You should eat something."

"I'm not hungry, and I was just going to the back veranda for some fresh air. Not that it's any of your business," Felicity replied coolly, pulling her wrist from Luke's grasp and heading out.

Felicity sat down on the large bench swing seat, breathing in the fresh country air, her eyes wandering over the beautiful Colorado countryside. She finished her coffee, lifted her legs up, curled them beneath her, and let the sway of the swing comfort her. She didn't feel her eyes close as exhaustion from her head injury had her sliding into sleep, yet again.

Felicity screamed at James as he grabbed her. "Let me go, you son of a bitch." Instead of letting her go, he slammed his mouth down

on hers, thrusting his hips into her stomach. She whimpered as she
struggled to free herself, then gagged as the bastard shoved his
tongue down her throat. She bit down hard on his tongue. She had just
enough time to turn her head, spit his blood from her mouth, before
pain exploded across her mouth and cheek as he slapped her. She
cried out as her head hit the timber on the side of the stall. His hands
gripped her shirt, ripping it open, exposing her breasts to his
lecherous eyes. She tried to kick and scratch him. She saw his fist
coming from her peripheral vision and knew she was in real deep
trouble.

"Felicity, wake up," a loud voice demanded.

Felicity opened her eyes, still whimpering as the remnants of her dream slowly faded away. She became aware of the fact that she was sitting on Sheriff Luke Sun-Walker's lap, his arms banded around her arms and waist as he rocked her gently. Tears were still streaming down her cheeks. Felicity tried to bury her head into Luke's chest to hide her fear and embarrassment from him, but he wouldn't let her. He moved her back slightly and gently lifted her eyes up to his. She caught sight of Tom and Billy sitting on either side and knew they had seen her tears. She took a few deep breaths, getting her emotions back under control, and wiped the tears from her cheeks as Luke loosened his hold on her. Then she lowered her head again.

"Sorry."

"You have nothing to be sorry for, baby. None of this was your fault," Tom stated firmly.

"I must have done something to make him think I wanted his touch. I think I should leave. I can get a job anywhere," Felicity said with a shudder.

"You will not be leaving from this ranch. You signed a twelve-month contract, and I'm not letting you break it," Tom replied, his voice hard as steel.

Felicity knew she didn't have a leg to stand on. She had signed that contract, and if she broke it, her two employers had every right to sue her for breaching it. She felt utterly mortified that she hadn't tried to get off Luke's lap and pushed against his arms, surprised when he let her go immediately. She turned to face the three men on the bench swing to apologize again for the trouble she'd caused with James. She didn't say anything. The three men were staring at her with so much heat and hunger in their eyes she felt a blush creep up over her cheeks, heating her bruised flesh. She opened her mouth to say something, snapped it closed again when words failed her, turned on her heel, and stormed back inside.

* * * *

Felicity recovered over the next few days. She was feeling much better and wanted to get back to work. Her employers and the sheriff wouldn't let her until she had the all clear from Doc. Felicity had no idea why the sheriff was staying at the Double E Ranch, but didn't think it was any of her business, so she didn't ask.

Felicity felt as if she was going stir crazy by the end of the week. She had a bad case of cabin fever. She wanted, no, needed to get out of the house and off the front porch before she blew a fuse. She knew Tom and Billy were in their office catching up on paperwork and the sheriff was in town at work. She quietly walked into the kitchen, told Nanette she was going to drive to town for a few female necessities, and took off. She gave a sigh of relief, her tension draining away for the first time in a week. The three men currently residing in the ranch house were beginning to get to her, and she was looking forward to the time away from them. Every time they came within reach, they would stroke her hair, arms or back. She was becoming sexually frustrated and relished the idea of an afternoon of freedom. She wondered what they would do if they knew she was beginning to crave their touch. Probably run away after she gave them what they wanted. She wasn't stupid enough to think they wanted any more from her than her body. She was just as determined not to give in to them.

Felicity had been raised by an elderly aunt, after the death of her parents in a boating accident. Felicity had been so young she couldn't even remember her parents. Of course she had photos of them, but she couldn't actually remember them herself. Her Aunt Sally had been fifteen years older than her mom and hadn't had an affectionate bone in her body. She had given Felicity every materialistic thing she had ever needed, but the one thing she had pined for had never been forthcoming from her spinster aunt. She had never hugged her or told her she loved her. By the time Felicity's aunt had died at the age of sixty-five, Felicity had just turned seventeen. Felicity had thought she would always have a home with her aunt, but had been surprised to find out the elderly woman had been destitute on death. Unbeknownst to Felicity, her Aunt Sally had spent her days at a casino, gambling away her money. She realized Aunt Sally must have been as lonely as Felicity had felt and had tried to compensate the lack of people in her life with the thrill of gambling. If Felicity had known, she may have made more of an effort to touch her aunt's heart.

Felicity pushed her thoughts away as she pulled into the parking lot of the local pharmacy. She collected the items every female needed, paid for them, then decided to take a stroll up and down the main street. She looked into shop windows, sighing over feminine clothing items she knew she would never have the chance to wear. She was heading back on the opposite side of the street and saw the local diner was open. She pushed the door open, entered, and took a seat in a secluded booth. She ordered a glass of lemonade as she watched the citizens of Slick Rock, Colorado, go about their daily chores. She had always loved the country and knew there was no way she would ever survive living in the city again. She hated the hustle and bustle of the city, as well as the smog and garbage, which always seemed to be strewn about.

Felicity had just finished her glass of lemonade when she saw the sheriff's car pull into a parking space outside the diner. She wondered what he was doing here. She watched him get out of his truck and scan the interior of the diner, his gaze stopping on her. He pinned her with his eyes as he walked toward the door. Felicity could tell by his gaze and clenched jaw as he strolled toward her that she was in trouble for something. Luke didn't take the seat across from her like she expected. He scooted her across the seat and sat beside her.

"What the hell do you think you're doing?" he snapped out, glaring at her.

"I was just having a drink. What does it look like I was doing?"

"Don't you get sassy with me, little girl, or I'll put you over my knee and smack your ass."

"I beg your pardon?" Felicity asked in her most haughty tone.

"You heard me, Felicity. Don't try my patience any more than you already have. Now, what are you doing in town?"

"I had to get some tampons from the pharmacy, Sheriff, not that it's any of your business what I do."

"Now, that's where you're wrong. You are my business. Did you have the courtesy to let Tom or Billy know where you were going or how long you would be? I'd think with that bastard still missing, you'd want people to know where you are in case he comes after you again."

"I let Nanette know where I was going. I can't believe you. What gives you the right to order me around? I've never had to answer to anyone before, and I'm not going to start now." Felicity hissed through clenched teeth.

"That's where you're wrong, Felicity. Everything you do is my, Tom's, and Billy's business. You agreed to abide by the rules when you signed that contract, sweetheart. Next time you want or need to go anywhere, you let one of us know. It's time to go back home. And since I've finished my shift, you're coming with me," Luke commanded. He manacled his hand around her wrist, pulled her up with him, without hurting her, dropped a few bills on the table, and led her out to his truck.

Felicity didn't try to dig her heels in since she was no match for such a strong, tall, forceful man. She loved the feel of his hands on her and wondered what she was thinking. How could she lust after three men at once? He had her strapped into the front seat of his truck before she could protest.

"Hey. What about my car? How am I going to get it back to the ranch?" Felicity whined as she watched her car disappear.

"Jack and one of the hands will get it later," Luke replied.

Felicity was so angry with his high-handed tactics she crossed her arms over her chest and stared out the passenger-side window, refusing to speak.

When Luke pulled the car up near the ranch house, Felicity got out of his truck, slammed the door, and ran inside. She didn't get very far. Tom and Billy must have heard them arrive. They were waiting inside the back door when she stormed in. Much to Felicity's dismay, Tom picked her up, slung her over his shoulder, and carried her into the study. He gently lowered her to the sofa, moved back away from her, and stood with him arms folded across his chest. Billy was leaning on the desk, and Luke entered the room a few moments later. They stood staring at her, anger evident in their eyes and their offensive stances. Their arms were crossed over their chests, their hips thrust forward, and they were all watching her with predatory intent.

"Who the fuck do you three think you are? What gives you the right to tell me what I can and can't do?" Felicity asked in a loud, indignant voice. She watched cautiously as Tom turned to his desk, opened a drawer, pulled a paper out, and stalked toward her.

"Felicity, did you even stop to think that James is still on the loose?" Tom asked quietly. "We have no idea where he is. He could have come after you in town. Don't you realize we're only trying to keep you safe? What were you doing in town?"

"I needed to buy a few things," Felicity replied, lowering her eyes from the three men.

"What did you need so desperately that you couldn't come and tell

Billy or me where you were going?" Tom asked.

Felicity didn't answer the question or even acknowledge the three men in the room. She didn't want them all knowing what she had gone to town to buy, even though it had just been an excuse to get out for a while. It was bad enough she had already blurted it out to Luke, trying to embarrass him, but instead ending up embarrassing herself in the process.

Tom wasn't going to let her get away without answering though. He moved to the sofa, sat down beside her, and gently took her chin between his thumb and finger, turning her head toward him. "Answer the question, Lis, or I'll put you over my knee."

"My name isn't Lis. It's Felicity. I needed some more tampons, all right? Are you happy now that you've humiliated me?"

"It was never my intention to humiliate you, Lis. I just need to know you're safe, since James hasn't been caught yet. We care about you and your welfare, and while you are on this ranch you will abide by our rules."

"I'm not a child. I've been looking after myself for four years. I don't need anyone watching out for me."

"I don't care. While you're on my ranch, you are under our protection. Now, I'm sure Nanette is wondering where we are. Dinner was ready about ten minutes ago. Come on, let's go eat," Tom stated as he rose to his feet. He held out his hand to Felicity, waiting to pull her to her feet.

"I'm not hungry."

"If you're not acting like a child, then why are you sulking?" Luke asked as he moved toward her.

Felicity watched him move with predatory grace. She felt her body warming from the inside out as he moved toward her. He gently tugged on her ponytail, tilting her head up to meet his sinful brown eyes. "You will go into that dining room and eat what Nanette has prepared. You will hurt her feelings if you don't."

"*Okay*," Felicity sighed, ignoring the three men and stomping to the dining room.

* * * *

"She is so fucking sexy. I can't wait to make her ours," Billy
stated. Luke nearly laughed when he saw his friend licking his lips.

"I know, bro, but it looks like we're gonna have to wait a few
more days. You know what women are like when they have their
monthly," Tom stated.

Luke knew his two friends were looking forward to punishing
their little woman for leaving the ranch without letting them know she
was leaving or taking anyone with her as much as he was. Their brand
of punishment would have left the four of them totally satisfied, but
now he had to put their plans on the back burner. He followed their
woman into the dining room.

Luke's eyes immediately landed on Felicity. She was sitting at the
table in between Jack and one of the other ranch hands, Spencer. He
didn't like the fact she was not near him, Tom, or Billy, but he didn't
want to make a scene, which he knew would end up in another
argument with their woman. He watched her talking to Jack and felt a
stab of jealousy at their easy camaraderie. He wanted to be able to
talk to her and have her conversing with him in such an easy manner.
He took a seat across from her, watching as she kept her eyes averted
from him, Tom, and Billy. Yep, she was sulking, and it looked like she
was going to continue giving them the cold shoulder. They couldn't
let her get away with that. Luke decided it was time to start training
their woman to let her know that she was theirs, and only theirs. They
didn't have to fuck her. They could bring her pleasure without even
penetrating her. He turned his head to Tom and Billy. Since the three
of them had practically grown up together, they often knew what the
other was thinking. Tom gave a barely perceptible nod, letting him
know he was in accordance with him.

Luke knew Tom was getting mighty pissed off at being ignored.
He and his friends hated it when a woman used the cold-shoulder,

silent treatment. He'd rather have a rip-roaring argument than be totally ignored because he knew that making up would be so sweet. Since he was still getting to know their little woman and wanted to know how she would react to being goaded, he decided that he, Tom, and Billy should begin their courting in earnest. Since Tom was sitting too far away to be able to touch Felicity and Billy had a ranch hand between him and Felicity, he knew he was the only one able to touch her without anyone else knowing. He nodded to Tom, letting him know the game was on.

Chapter Four

Felicity froze in her seat when she felt a large socked foot sliding up her calf. She flinched, trying to keep her cheeks from heating with embarrassment. Jack turned to look at her curiously and, when he saw her heated cheeks, must have thought she wasn't feeling well.

"Are you all right, Felicity?"

"Fine," she squeaked out. She cleared her throat and repeated her answer in a calmer voice. "I'm fine, thanks, Jack."

"You look a little flushed, sweetheart. Are you sure you're all right?"

"Yeah, just a little tired, I guess," Felicity answered. She turned away from Jack and glared at Luke.

Felicity could see Luke was struggling not to smile. She could see the twinkle of amusement in his eyes. She felt him slide his foot a little higher, keeping his eyes on hers the whole time. His foot was now in between her thighs, halfway between her knee and pussy. Felicity gave Luke her best "you're dead" stare from across the table. She felt him slip his foot up higher until he was covering her pussy with his large appendage. She nearly groaned out loud from sheer pleasure as she felt the moist heat of her cunt being touched through her jeans. She loved being touched by Luke, Tom, and Billy. She was just anxious about being caught by the others. She jumped to her feet and stood glaring at him.

"Are you all right, honey? Can I get you something?" Nanette asked from across the kitchen counter.

"Um, I just wanted to get a glass of water," Felicity replied, looking to Nan.

"There's a jug on the table already, honey. There should be glasses, too. Yes, there they are, behind the jug. Luke, pour Felicity some water," Nanette demanded then returned to cleaning the kitchen.

Felicity reluctantly returned to her chair but didn't pull herself as close to the table. Hopefully she was thwarting Luke by not moving in so close to him, but he was such a tall man, she knew she didn't have much chance of keeping him and his foot at bay. Not that she really wanted to. She was fighting the urge to crawl over the table, sit in his lap, and place his big hands on her breast and pussy. She wondered what the hell he thought he was doing. Why was he hitting on her? She looked to Tom and Billy to see if they had been watching. She glared at them as they gave her innocent smiles. Oh yeah, they knew. She wasn't that ignorant of men. She did read erotic romance novels, after all. Even though she was still a virgin, she knew what went on between men and women. Felicity ate a few mouthfuls of food, not really tasting anything. She was just beginning to relax again when she felt Luke's foot in her crotch. He hadn't given her any warning this time. He had gone straight for what he wanted. Felicity jumped to her feet, grabbed her plate, and took it into the kitchen.

"Thanks for dinner, Nanette. I'm sorry I couldn't do it justice. I'm just not very hungry," Felicity stated, and then she practically ran for her bedroom.

* * * *

Nan turned to Luke, Tom, and Billy. She stood with her hands on her ample hips, tapping her foot on the floor, and glared at the three men. "What did you do to that poor girl? She ran out of the room as if all the hounds of hell were on her heels."

"We didn't do anything," Tom replied, struggling to keep his amusement from showing.

"And pigs fly backwards. I know you three, and I know what you're up to. You treat that little girl right. She's an innocent little thing, and if you hurt her, you'll be answering to me."

"Yes, ma'am," they all replied, lowering their eyes to their plates, continuing their meal.

* * * *

Felicity sighed with relief, the tension in her body easing as she gathered her large sleeping shirt then headed to the shower. When she finished her shower, she dried off and began to dry her hair. Her hair was so long it reached the top of her ass. She loved having long hair. It made her feel feminine while she was working in such a male-dominated industry. She had nearly cut it off once, knowing it would be easier to take care of, not take so long to dry, but to her, it was her only feminine attribute. When she was working, she kept it tied up and out of the way, but when she was alone, she loved the feel of it sliding over her skin. She finished drying her hair, and picked up her favorite body butter. Felicity made sure to moisturize her skin every night after spending all day outside in the elements. She loved the Frangipani scent emanating from her warm skin after she was clean. It was another nightly ritual she loved, that helped to remind herself she was a woman. She spent all her time around men being one of the boys all day, every day. So she loved to pamper herself at night, away from prying eyes.

Felicity had been on her own for so long now, she had no idea how to let anyone else take control. She often dreamed about having a man to lean on, to take care of her so she could relinquish control to him, but she knew that would never happen. She had become too independent. She'd had to. It was either that or not survive the harsh realities of life. She had been on her own for four years, since the age of seventeen. Thinking back over the years with her aunt, she realized she had been self-sufficient for far longer than four years. She never had any hugs or love from her aunt. She didn't think the woman knew how to show emotion. She had been so cold to her. Maybe she had begrudged having to take care of a child that wasn't of her own body, but then she had known her aunt was a dried-up spinster. She'd had no friends in her life, and she hadn't allowed Felicity to bring friends home with her or go and visit friends after school. Felicity had never celebrated a birthday or been given a gift in remembrance of her birth. Her aunt would hand her a card without saying a word, and then she would go about her day. More often than not, it was Felicity who did the cooking and cleaning at her aunt's house.

She wondered how long her aunt had had a gambling problem. Looking back, she knew it must have been for years. The woman was only ever home in the evenings, expecting Felicity to have a meal on the table when she walked in the door. She couldn't remember a time before her seventh birthday when she had not been doing most of the housework for her aunt. The day she had turned eight was the day her cooking lessons began. Her aunt had never scolded her for some of the disasters she had cooked, but she knew she had not been happy. It had been there in her eyes and the set of her mouth. Felicity had begun to query herself, why she was such a difficult child to love. She had done everything within her power to please her aunt, but her efforts were wasted. Therefore, she had learned not to become attached to anyone. She began to push her friends away, knowing it was a useless endeavor to have them since she was never allowed over to play or have them over to her aunt's house.

Felicity sighed as she climbed into bed. At least she had never been bored. She learned to fill in her spare time with books. Her love of reading had kept her sane. Felicity reached over to the bedside table, pulled out the erotic romance she had picked up in town, and settled down to lose herself within the pages.

Felicity was so engrossed in her dream world when she heard the footsteps stop at her bedroom door, she ignored it. She caught movement from the corner of her eye and jerked with surprise to see three men standing in her bedroom, observing her as the door closed behind them.

* * * *

Luke stood watching their woman. She was so enthralled in her book she was unaware of their presence. The cover on the book caught Luke's attention. He couldn't hold back his grin of delight as he studied the two men and one woman on the cover of the book. It looked like their woman was into reading about ménages. This was going to make their job of training their woman to accept the loving of three men a lot easier.

Luke wasn't sure which one of them had made a sound, but Felicity looked up and stared as she saw them standing in her bedroom. She moved like lightning, hiding her book beneath the bed covers as she gaped at them, her mouth hanging open. She quickly snapped her mouth shut, swallowed loudly, and then changed her facial expression to a scowl as he stood watching her.

"What the fuck are you doing in my room? Get out, now," she said without any emphasis, but Luke could see the desire in her eyes as she ran them over his body. He watched Felicity's chest rise and fall as her breathing increased. He saw her nipples harden under her shirt, and she wriggled with desire as she stared at them. Their little baby was turned on.

"No," Luke replied as he stalked toward her.

"What? What do you want? I think you should leave. Nan could catch you in here."

"No. Nan's gone home," Tom replied.

* * * *

Felicity had a fair idea what was going on, and the heated looks they were giving her as the three men moved to stand at the end of the bed had her squirming with arousal. She was so attracted to the three men. Her breasts felt heavy, and her pussy was beginning to leak out juices. They had teased her with their heated stares and sexy looks. They had touched her every time she walked past them, a hand on her hip, her back, her arm, and even a slight brush of an arm to her breast, if the opportunity arose.

"I knew your hair would be long. You look so sexy, baby," Tom said then licked his lips.

"Oh, my God," Felicity squeaked. "What do you want?" Felicity asked, trying to appear belligerent to hide her arousal, and crossed her arms over her breasts.

"You," Luke replied heatedly.

"What? No, you don't want me. Besides you can't," Felicity stated, licking her lips.

"Oh, you're killing me, honey," Luke groaned out.

Felicity jerked as they moved forward together. Luke and Tom walked to either side of the bed, and Billy began to crawl up the mattress. She pushed the covers back, her feet on the floor, not wanting to make it easy for the three men. *Shit, I'm falling for them. God, I want them so much.*

"Then what the hell are you waiting for? Come and get me, big boy," Felicity goaded as she tried to stand. She never made it to her feet. Luke pounced on her since he was the closest. He took her down to the mattress with him, covering her mouth with his own. He grasped her wrists in his large hands and pulled her arms up above her head. He manacled them in one large hand. He devoured her mouth with his own.

Felicity couldn't prevent the groan from escaping her mouth as Luke slowed and gentled the kiss. She moaned as Luke pressed his hips into hers. He took advantage and swept his tongue into her mouth, sliding it against hers, tilting his head for the optimum access to her mouth. He explored every nook and cranny of her mouth. Sliding his tongue up to the roof, tickling her palette, then along the inside of her cheeks, over her teeth, along her lower lip, then back to duel his tongue with hers. She was on fire. Felicity felt liquid pooling between her thighs, making her pussy throb with unrequited desire. Her lower abdomen was heavy, cramping, her cunt begging to be filled. She had never been kissed with such intensity or felt such avid passion. It was frightening, but so good. She felt the mattress dip on either side of her and knew Tom and Billy were at her sides. What were they doing to her? She couldn't keep a thought in her head. They flitted in then out at a rapid pace. Then there were no thoughts at all.

* * * *

Luke was in heaven and hell. The first taste of Felicity had him losing control. He thrust his tongue in and out of her mouth, tasting her female desire. He wanted to strip her naked and plunge into her tight, wet heat, but knew that wasn't an option. He weaned his mouth from hers, raised his head, and looked down into her flushed face. Her lips were so red and full from his kisses, and he imagined them wrapped around his cock. He growled as she opened her eyes. They were a deep, dark blue, almost violet, and her pupils were dilated with the passion he had aroused in her. He slipped a knee between her legs then sat up on his knees, pulling her into a sitting position with him. He clasped her hands in one of his behind her back, causing her to arch her spine, thrusting her breasts out to him. He used his free hand to pull the large baggy shirt up over her head, using the shirt to trap her arms by holding it behind her back with her arms still trapped in the fabric.

He stared down at her voluptuous chest. Her breasts were high on her chest, her nipples a light pink color, which made him salivate to get his mouth on one of those hard tips. He leaned down, licked her nipple with the flat of his tongue, and then sucked it into his mouth. He lapped on her nipple firmly, his free hand at her hip, holding her in place. He couldn't get enough of her. He moved his hand down to her pussy, cupping her cunt, enveloping it with his large palm. He lifted his head from her breast, and he watched her body jerk as she climaxed. It was one of the most beautiful sights he had ever seen in his whole life. He eased his hand away from her pussy, knowing if he didn't pull back he would be stripping her naked, fucking her regardless of her having her period. Luke moved off to the side to let his friend in to take over Felicity's pleasure.

* * * *

Tom picked her up and pulled her onto his lap so she was straddling his thighs, the front of her body facing his. He pulled the large shirt off her arms and placed his hands at the sides of her face, careful not to touch her bruises, holding her still as he gazed into her eyes. He held her eyes to his, not letting her pull back or look away from him as he slowly lowered his head to hers. He didn't close his eyes as his mouth first touched hers. He licked his lips along the seam of hers, asking permission to take things further. He slid his lips over hers, angling his head to cover her mouth completely. He watched her pupils dilate as he controlled the kiss they shared. He felt her lips open as she gasped air into her lungs, and taking advantage, he thrust his tongue into her mouth. Her moan as she capitulated to his dominance had his hard cock pulsing against the zipper of his jeans. He watched as her eyes closed, her body softening into his as she gave him what he wanted. Complete and utter control over her pleasure.

Tom ravaged Felicity's mouth with his own, thrusting his tongue into her mouth, entwining it with hers. He pulled back slightly, nibbling on her full lower lip, causing her to moan into his mouth. He sucked on her flesh then thrust his tongue back into her depths. He curled his tongue around hers, drawing it from her mouth into his own.

He suckled on her flesh, making her sob with passion. He moved one of his hands down to her waist, stroking her warm, soft, silky flesh with his palm and fingers. He slowly slid his hand up to over her stomach until he reached the underside of her breast. His palm flattened over her ribs, his fingers long enough to touch the underside of her fleshy mound. He rubbed his thumb back and forth underneath her soft globe.

He needed to feel her breast filling his hand, her nipple jutting into his palm. He moved up, enveloping her in his hand, kneading her soft, voluptuous skin. Her little pink-tipped nipple firmed beneath his touch, stabbing at him for more. He pinched her turgid peak between his thumb and finger, making her cry into his mouth once more. He moved his free hand down over her stomach until he reached the elastic at the top of her panties. He wanted to thrust his fingers into her cunt, wanted to see her ride his hand until she climaxed, but didn't want to scare her off. So instead he slipped his hand beneath the elastic until he felt the little nub of flesh at the top of her pussy with his large finger.

He pulled his hand from her panties, weaned his mouth from her own, and lifted his finger to his mouth as she watched him through heavy eyelids. He sucked his finger into his mouth, and when he pulled it out, he made sure he had saliva coating his digit. He slipped his hand back under the material of her panties and began massaging his finger over her engorged clit. He leaned down and forward, taking one of her nipples into his mouth. He sucked on her nipple, dragging it between his teeth, flicking his tongue over her hard peak until she was arching into his mouth and rocking her hips into his hand. He slid his hand to her lower belly, just above the top of her cunt, over her pubic mound.

He pushed down on her resolutely then moved his hand around in slow massaging circles. He pressed his finger more firmly over her sensitive clit as he swirled and rubbed over her nerve endings. He could feel her stomach jumping and trembling beneath his hand and knew Felicity was close to reaching orgasm. He gently grazed his teeth over her nipple, slipped his thumb into her panties with his finger, and gently pinched her clitoris between the two.

He opened his eyes, looked up, and watched as his woman threw her head back as she screamed out her release. Tom pulled his hand from her panties and his mouth from her breast, pulled her onto his lap, and held her as she quavered and trembled in his arms. She finally slumped against his body, totally relaxed for the first time since he, Luke, and Billy had entered her room. The only sound was the harsh, rapid breaths of all four adults.

Tom felt a drop of moisture hit his chest, then another and another, until he realized it wasn't sweat like he had believed. Felicity was crying quietly in his arms, and he had no idea why. He was about to find out though. He hoped they hadn't scared her by coming on too strong with their feisty but submissive little woman. He eased her back from his chest so he could see her face, but she kept her head down, using her hair to hide her face. He tilted her face up to his with a knuckle then, using his free hand, he brushed her hair back from her face.

"Open your eyes and look at me, baby," Tom demanded. He would have laughed at her petulance when she scrunched her eyes tighter, her lower lip protruding into a pout, but he didn't want to humiliate her and have her closing herself off from him, his brother, and his friend. He needed for Felicity to feel comfortable with them and come to them if she was upset or had a problem. "Now, Felicity."

Chapter Five

Felicity finally opened her eyes and looked at Tom through her tears. She didn't want to look but knew if she didn't obey him, she would be in deep trouble, and that's just what she wanted. They were all such dominant men. When they commanded or demanded, they expected to be obeyed immediately. She looked at Tom anxiously as he studied her face.

"Why are you crying?"

Felicity didn't even know herself, so how the hell could he demand she explain it to him? "I don't know," she replied with a shrug of her shoulders, lowering her eyelashes to hide her bewilderment.

Tom wouldn't let her get away with not looking at him. He smacked her lightly on the thigh, making her flinch with surprise and look at him in obfuscation. "Don't look away from me when I'm talking to you. Now, tell me why you were crying."

"I don't know." Felicity wailed, tears leaking from the corner of her eyes again.

Felicity felt the mattress dip behind her. Legs moved along beside hers, and a large, warm, masculine chest cuddled against her back. She turned her head to see Billy leaning over her body. He placed a comforting kiss on the naked skin of her shoulder then leaned his chin on her. Luke moved in from the side, took her hand in his, and began to rub her thigh in soothing strokes. She was surrounded by warmth, comfort, and affection. She'd never felt so protected in her life. It was too much to handle for someone who had never been cuddled or cared for. It was the catalyst that shattered the ice encasing her heart. She began to sob in earnest, and once she started, she couldn't stop.

She cried for the parents she never knew, for the lack of friends and companions she'd had to turn away over the years. She cried for her lonely, dried-up, spinster aunt who couldn't show her how to love, and most of all, she cried for herself. She cried for all the loneliness and the lack of human contact throughout her entire life. Finally her tears slowed and stopped. She gave a few hiccups until she could finally breathe more easily. One of the men handed her some tissues, so she blew her nose, keeping her head lowered. She was so embarrassed over the way she had fallen apart and now understood why she had been crying, but she wanted to try and hide it from them. She needed to wrap herself up in that ice again, because if she didn't she knew she would end up totally shattered.

"Look at me, baby," Tom commanded again.

Felicity didn't bother trying to hide this time. She could hear the frustration in Tom's voice and didn't want to give him any cause to be angry with her.

"Why were you crying?"

Felicity didn't answer. She lowered her eyelashes once more, giving a negligible shrug of her shoulders.

"I am not going to push you any more tonight, but be warned. From now on, you are our woman. You will not deny me, Billy, or Luke anything. If we ask you a question, you will answer immediately. If you have any problems, you will come to one of us and talk it through. If one of us upsets you, you will talk it out with that person and let them know how you feel. If you can't resolve the problem between you and the other person, you will bring another of us in to act as mediator. You will not leave this ranch without telling one of us where you are going, how long you will be, and if necessary, you will take one of us with you. Do you understand what I am telling you?" Tom asked.

Felicity couldn't believe what he had just stated. He had said she was their woman. Did that mean she was going to be available to all three of them when they wanted to fuck? She jumped from the bed, grabbed her shirt, and pulled it over her head. She stood glaring at the three men looking at her expectantly.

"Are you out of your fucking mind?" Felicity yelled. "How dare you tell me what I can and can't do. How dare you think I'll be a quick roll in the hay for you to relieve an itch. Who the hell do you think you are? I don't answer to you or anyone else. God, your ego is so big it's a wonder your head hasn't exploded."

Felicity let her eyes rake over the three men staring at her from the bed as she stopped her ranting. She watched as their eyes changed from astonishment to anger in the blink of her eye. Uh-oh. She was in deep shit. She spun on her heels, slammed into the bathroom, and locked the door. She covered her mouth as a hysterical giggle threatened to erupt. The look on Tom's face as she slammed and locked the door before he could reach her was not pleasant. In fact, it was downright furious. She was contemplating if it would be in her best interests to pack up her car and steal away in the night. The thought of leaving the Double E Ranch, but more importantly the three men living in the ranch house, sent a shard of pain piercing through her heart.

In spite of everything, she knew she was falling in love with them. *Oh no, please no.* She didn't want to be in love with those three men. They would break her heart. She knew there was no way in hell she would survive having her heart shattered by them. She was going to have to leave. She sat down on the closed toilet lid in defeat. She was going to miss them so much. She had no idea when they had crept in under her skin and taken her heart into the palm of their hands. Maybe she could get Jack to help her. He was such a nice man. They had become good friends practically from the first day she had arrived on the Double E Ranch. Yeah, Jack would help her sneak out.

Felicity had heard the three men stomp out of her bedroom, but she was cautious and peeked through a gap in the door before exiting the bathroom. She began to pack up her stuff and hid what she could in the closets and bathroom. If everything went according to plan, maybe she wouldn't need to ask Jack for help after all. The more she thought about it, the more she was determined to leave in the early hours of the morning. It was better if she didn't talk to Jack since he was the ranch foreman. Even though she liked him and he seemed to like her, because he was in charge of the ranch hands, he might get it into his head to let his bosses know what she was up to.

Once Felicity had everything organized, she slid into bed, hoping to catch a couple of hours sleep before she could sneak her belongings to her car. Not that she had much stuff, but someone would definitely notice her forays in and out of the house with her couple of boxes and case of clothing. If she encountered anyone, she would act as if nothing was wrong. She would have to figure out what to tell them about her being up and about in the early hours, if she got caught. But she didn't think she would have any problems. She planned to be well and truly on her way by 3:00 a.m. It should be a piece of cake.

Then why the hell did she feel so miserable?

* * * *

"Do you have any idea what the hell that was about?" Luke asked as he sat on the living room sofa drinking coffee.

"No. Has she said anything to you, Billy?" Tom asked.

"Nope. I mean, what the hell? It looked like she was so full of pain, like her heart was breaking, with her crying so much. I wish she would open up and talk to us. God, who knew it would be so hard to start courting a woman?" Billy asked.

"She's only really been seen talking to Jack. Maybe we should call him over from the bunkhouse, see if he knows anything about her," Tom queried.

"I'll go get him," Billy stated.

Luke watched as his friend's long legs ate up the distance to the back door rapidly. He wasn't surprised when Billy was back ten minutes later, Jack at his side. The two men took seats and looked at him then Tom.

"Thanks for coming over, Jack. We have a few questions to ask you regarding Felicity. Does she talk to you much besides ranch business?" Tom asked.

Luke saw Jack relax back into his seat, and knew the man had been concerned over being asked up to the house. Luke and his friends began trying to pump Jack for information about Felicity. He admired the way Jack took his time to think over his thoughts before he began to speak.

"I know her parents died when she was just a toddler. I asked her about them one day, and she said she couldn't remember her parents and went on to explain why. She didn't tell me how they died though."

"Can you remember anything else?" Luke asked, leaning forward, waiting for a reply.

"I think she said an elderly maiden aunt raised her, but she didn't go into any detail. Oh, she's been on her own since she was seventeen. That I do remember. I thought it was way too young for a female to have to be alone. Can I enquire why all the questions?" Jack asked curiously.

"We want to claim her as ours. We laid down the law to her tonight, and she got upset. Her tears were nearly more than we could bear. Then she had the audacity to yell at us and lock herself in the bathroom," Billy stated. Luke watched in amazement as Jack threw his head back and burst out laughing.

"I'm sorry. I know it probably doesn't seem funny to you, but I just had a picture of that tiny woman going at you then storming off in a temper. She's such a feisty little thing. She can be so cool and controlled, but when her temper gets the better of her, boy, she nearly singes you with her fire."

"Hmm, I think you've hit on something there, Jack. Thanks for coming over and talking to us," Luke said then shook Jack's hand.

Tom and Billy rose to their feet, thanking him and shaking Jack's hand as well. Luke watched the foreman leave, the man still chuckling every now and then, shaking his head, until he was gone, exiting the back door, closing it behind him.

"You know, what Jack said makes sense. I think our little Flick has been hurt badly in the past. She has built walls so high around herself, trying to keep people out. She is so full of passion, but I don't think she even knows it. I have a feeling she's buried her true self and has no idea who she is inside. I think we need to break down those walls she's built up as protection. We are going to have to be there when those walls come tumbling down. There is no way in hell I'm letting another man near her when her true self begins to show," Luke stated.

Luke had decided Flick was an apt nickname for their woman, as she was always flicking her ponytail back off her shoulders and because he knew she liked it. Every time he called her Flick, she'd smile and toss back her bound hair again. He sometimes saw sadness in her eyes, too, and wondered why. He wanted to ask her, but he wanted her to come to him and tell him why she was sad at times.

"I think you may be right, Luke. Those tears are a testament that we're getting to her. I believe she honestly doesn't know what she's feeling. But how the hell do we break down those walls?" Tom asked.

"I think we've already taken the first step to doing that. She broke down for no apparent reason, and then she used anger to keep us at arm's length when you told her our rules. She was trying to gather those walls back up around her heart," Billy stated.

"When did you get to be so wise, little bro?" Tom asked with a grin.

"You'd be surprised what I've learned from women over the years," Billy said with a chuckle.

"I've got a sinking feeling in my gut, and since my gut instincts have never let me down before, we need to keep an eye on Felicity. I think she's gonna try and leave. I can't tell you why I think that, it's just intuition," Luke said.

"I think I need to have a look at the car we have under the carport," Tom said.

Luke looked at his friend as he rose to his feet and tried to figure out what Tom was going to do. He finally realized Tom wanted to make sure Felicity's car was safe for her to drive. Luke and his friends whispered to each other as they worked on Felicity's car. They made sure it was safe for her in case she wanted to go to town, with their permission, of course. Luke wanted to replace her old car with a brand new one, but knew Felicity would put up a fuss. He wondered how the old, rusted-out vehicle was still able to start. When he and his friends had done as much as they could, they crept back inside, washed up, and went to bed.

Chapter Six

Felicity was glad her internal alarm clock was still right on time. Her eyes popped open at 2:30 a.m., and instead of being groggy with sleep, she was wide awake. She rose from the bed, dressed quickly, went to the bathroom and brushed her teeth and hair. She collected the last of her belongings, shoved them in her bag, and crept to her bedroom door. She listened carefully, making sure everyone was asleep. She could hear quiet snores coming from the two bedrooms next to hers, and she sighed in relief. She was going to have to be extremely quiet. She frowned, trying to remember if any of the timber floorboards creaked or groaned as she walked over them. She gave a mental shrug, as she had no idea. Since she hadn't planned on sneaking out until tonight, she hadn't taken any notice. Oh well, not much she could do about that now.

Felicity opened the bedroom door wide, walked back to the closet, retrieved the two small boxes of belongings, and then quietly crept down the long hallway. She was glad she had a pair of sneakers, as they were much quieter than boots. She was very careful to walk on the balls of her feet, not wanting to land too heavily with her heels. She leaned the two boxes against the timber doorframe of the back entrance then eased the exit open. Shit. She'd forgotten about the screen door. She placed her boxes on the floor, eased the door open, letting her breath rush out when the door didn't squeak, and reached up, using the O-ring to keep the screen door propped wide. She crept to the other end of the house along the gravel drive, but when able, she moved off the gravel to walk on the grass. She wanted to keep her footsteps light and muffled as much as possible. She eased the back door of her car open, placed the boxes on the far side of the seat, and then crept back into the house. She retrieved her small suitcase and purse and made sure she had her keys ready in her hand.

The stab of pain to her heart caught her unawares, and she had to bite the bottom lip of her mouth hard enough to draw blood so she wouldn't cry out. She took one last look around the bedroom, straightened her spine, and pushed her shoulders back, heading to the back door. She pulled the back door closed behind her, turning the knob so the latch wouldn't click into place loudly. She froze when she heard a squeak inside. When she heard no other sound, she put the noise down to the timber structure of the house cooling and shrinking in the early hours. She placed her case onto the decking, reached up, and released the O-ring. She eased the screen door back into the doorjamb then slowly released the handle back into place.

Felicity picked her case up and walked down the steps, lightly along the gravel drive and grass. She eased her case into the backseat and closed the back car door, easing it into place with a quiet snick. She got into the driver's seat, threw her purse onto the passenger seat, and put the key into the ignition. She released the handbrake, shifted the stick into reverse, took a deep breath, and turned the key in the ignition. Nothing happened. She turned the key and tried again, and again and again.

Felicity was biting her lip, with tears tracking down her cheeks, when the driver's side door was hauled open. She didn't have time to blink or take another breath before large, firm hands were hauling her out of her car. Felicity screamed with fear and shock as she was slung over a broad male shoulder. Her scream of fright was cut off when she realized who had her. She knew she was in trouble now. She had tried to leave, and in their eyes, she had broken the rules of their contract. She knew their brand of punishment was going to have her screaming in pleasure. She squirmed and squeezed her legs together, trying to relieve the ache in her pussy. A large hand came down on her ass, hard. The smack was enough to get her uncooperative lungs to fill with the precious oxygen she needed. She took a few big gulps of air then slumped in relief over the hard male shoulder. She felt dampness on her cheeks and realized she'd been crying as she fought to get air into her lungs. She knew deep down she was using her anger as a defense mechanism, but wasn't willing to reason out the cause of it just yet. She turned her head and knew it was Luke carrying her. "Where are you taking me?" Felicity asked as Luke carried her through the back door. He didn't even acknowledge she had spoken, just kept right on walking.

"Who do you think you are? I am going to report you to your superiors for kidnapping. Don't think I won't. You can't watch me twenty-four hours a day. Just you wait, you bastard. I am going to hand you your balls on a platter. I've been waiting for this. You have no idea how much," Felicity goaded as she slapped his back. When that didn't get a reaction, she grabbed onto his belt, pulled herself lower down his back, opened her mouth wide, and bit his ass, hard. She gave a satisfied smirk when he yelped in pain. She couldn't wait for her punishment. She was so turned on, and she knew Luke, Tom, and Billy would never lose control around her and hurt her.

Felicity went flying through the air. One minute she was upside down, biting Luke's ass, the next she was squealing as she flew. She landed on the large mattress in the bedroom she had been using with a soft thud and a bounce. She opened her eyes to see three very large, tall, pissed-off men. They stood glaring down at her, their arms crossed over their wide chests, their hips thrust forward with aggression. *Oh shit.* Even though she knew they would never hurt her, she didn't want the victory of their punishment to her to be too effortless. She saw them move out of the corner of her eye and knew her mouth was hanging open with shock. All three of them were stripping out of their clothes. Felicity rolled over to the other side of the bed until she was standing. She kept her eyes glued to the three men, heat creeping over her cheeks as they stood before her in all their naked glory. And glory it was. Their cocks were huge. She had never seen a cock in real life before, but she knew a stallion when she saw one. They were the perfect specimens of tall, muscular Adonises, and she couldn't seem to drag her eyes away from their bobbing, pulsing appendages.

They were all big, but they differed in size and length. The only thing they seemed to have in common was the reddish-purple color of the heads, which looked painful and angry. She closed her eyes with a whimper and swallowed hard. She knew they must have heard her loud gulp, and then she couldn't help a moan escaping from between her lips. She knew what they had in mind, like that was hard to figure out, but since she had never been with a man before, she was a bit apprehensive, but so damn horny she was beside herself with need.

Felicity didn't hear them move, but shrieked when warm, firm hands grabbed her by her upper arms and gently pushed her onto the bed. She didn't even get to twitch a muscle before two more sets of hands were holding her down and anchoring her to the bed. She felt her nipples harden and her pussy clench, dripping moisture onto her panties, making them damp. What the hell was wrong with her? Why the hell was she so turned on?

Felicity yelled with pleasure as firm hands grabbed her clothes and stripped them from her body. She was lying naked in front of men for the first time in her life. She felt as if all her shields had been ripped away from her. She had never felt so vulnerable, but she was so horny she could feel her juices leaking from her pussy onto her thighs. She bucked her hips up and twisted this way and that, trying to get them to touch her cunt. She didn't stand a chance. She screamed again with frustration as her arms were pulled above her head with some sort of restraints, and then her legs were given the same treatment. The only exceptions were her lower limbs, which had been spread wide before being secured in place.

She bucked and twisted, begging them to make love to her, tears coursing down her cheeks with her need. She felt the mattress dip in on either side of her as well as between her splayed thighs. She kept her eyes closed, not wanting to see the pity on their faces at her desperation.

She had decided since she didn't want to win, but didn't want to give in too easily, she would ignore them. She prayed her body didn't betray her too much and let them know they made her burn for their touch. But then she remembered she'd just begged them to love her. God, she was such a fool. She couldn't even hide how they made her feel.

"You can tell us anything. You are going to have to learn not to lie to us, Flick," Luke stated.

Felicity felt her heart clench as Luke inadvertently called her a liar. She remembered when she was small how she had accidentally broken one of her aunt's precious vases. She had accused Felicity of breaking it on purpose and had punished her by sending her to her room without supper. The memory was a catalyst, and her emotions bubbled to the surface. She bit her lower lip, drawing more blood as she tried to hold back emotions she'd buried for years.

"Fuck, sweetheart, stop biting yourself. You're bleeding," Billy stated.

Felicity didn't want concern for her welfare from them. She wanted to stay angry, knowing if they were to show her any form of sympathy she would break. She was so highly strung, and her muscles, tight, clenched, felt ready to snap from the least bit of provocation. She didn't want them to show any emotions at all. The touch of a gentle finger swiping the blood from her chin and lip sent her over the edge. She felt tears begin to leak from the corner of her eyes. The more she tried to stop them, the faster they fell. Her chest and throat felt tight, and she was having trouble breathing. There was a huge lump in her throat, and her heart was racing, pounding against the wall of her chest. Her heart skipped a beat then slammed twice as fast as it should have. She felt pain below her sternum, her life muscle leaping and pounding. The feeling scared the shit out of her, making her wonder if she was having a heart attack. The keening of a tortured voice sounded loudly in her ears. She wanted to cover them and block the sound out, but couldn't seem to move her arms. She tried to curl herself into a fetal position, trying to hold herself together, but couldn't seem to manage it.

Felicity knew she was falling apart, but couldn't seem to stop herself from splintering into a million pieces. She had been numb for so long, working herself into the ground, using her work to keep herself together. She finally realized she was the one making those horrible sounds. She had somehow managed to curl her body into itself as her mind and heart fell apart. She couldn't stop the sobs wracking her body or the tears streaming down her face. She didn't want to feel again. She'd tried to push her feelings and emotions to the back of her mind until she performed daily tasks in automation. She had been a breathing robot, not a female human being.

She was in her own private living hell, and the black hole was so deep she didn't think she would ever be able to climb out of it.

* * * *

"Billy, go call Doc. Tell him to hurry," Tom said in a tortured voice. He felt so helpless not being able to get through to Felicity. He saw the same tortured expressions on his brother's and friend's faces as well. They had no idea what was going on and no idea how to help their woman. They had never seen a woman so broken, in so much pain. He helped remove Felicity's restraints and watched Luke cover her with a blanket, his hands clenched into fists, his knuckles white.

Billy was back in seconds, and Tom watched his brother open his mouth to speak, stop, and clear his throat several times before he managed to form any words. "Doc, ten minutes."

Tom kept glancing at his watch. Every second felt like an hour. Every minute felt like a day. He walked over to Felicity and picked her up into his arms. He placed her on his lap and held her against him as he rocked her. He wasn't sure who he was trying to comfort more. He was torn up inside, seeing his woman in such a state, and hoped like hell they hadn't been the cause of such pain.

Tom saw Luke run to the door when he heard Doc pull up. He'd had his ears trained to listen for the man. His friend led Doc into the bedroom and stood back against the wall beside him, his muscles tight with fear that he, his brother, and his friend were the reason for Felicity's condition. He wanted to slam his fist into the walls, hurt himself for the pain their little woman was feeling, but knew to do so wouldn't make him feel any better. He, Luke, and Billy watched Doc administer a shot into Felicity's arm after swabbing her flesh with an alcohol wipe. He took her blood pressure then listened to her heart. He saw the frown form on Doc's face as the elderly man moved his stethoscope over her chest, then back to the region of her heart once more. He watched Doc lift her hand, turn it over so he could access the pulse point on her wrist, and time the beat of her heart against the second hand of his watch. Doc didn't move for a long time. He just sat on the side of the bed using the tools of his trade, all the while stroking a hand down over her head and hair.

Tom breathed a sigh of relief when Felicity's sobbing finally stopped and her breathing slowed, occasional hiccups making her shudder as she finally slipped into sleep. He watched as Doc removed his fingers from her wrist, pulled his stethoscope away from her chest, got up from the bed, and headed out to the kitchen. He took a seat at the large dining table and looked up to him, and Tom knew he had the same tortured expression on his face as Billy and Luke.

Tom could tell Doc was gathering his thoughts by the frown of concentration on his face. The elderly man watched him as Tom put the coffeepot on, the mundane task helping to keep his concerns under control.

"Felicity was having a panic attack. I think she's been bottling up emotion and pain for a long time. I don't know what you did to break through her reserves and I don't want to know." Doc paused, putting his hand up to stop any interruptions. "I'm just glad you did. That little girl was heading for a nervous breakdown. I don't want her working for at least two weeks. She is totally exhausted physically, but more so emotionally. I want one of you with her at all times. If you have any concerns at all, call me. If she shows signs of having another one of these episodes, call me. I don't care what time of day or night it is. If I'm not available one of the other doctors in the clinic will come out."

"Are you sure it wasn't our fault, Doc?" Luke asked.

"Yes, I'm sure," Doc replied, taking a sip of coffee from the mug Tom placed in front of him. "You three need to get that little girl to open up to you. She needs to get rid of those hurts she's got buried deep inside her. You need to really listen to what she says when she finally opens up. That little girl needs understanding and the love from all three of you."

Tom helped as Doc rose from his chair when he finished his coffee. He said good-bye to him, Billy, and Luke and drove away from the Double E Ranch.

Chapter Seven

Felicity woke up feeling like she'd been in a train wreck. Her body felt heavy, tired, and achy. Her face and eyes felt swollen and like she had sand beneath her eyelids. It took her a few moments to pry her glued eyelids open. She turned her head, looking around the room she had been sleeping in recently. She frowned, speculative over why she was still at the Double E Ranch. Memory slammed back into her brain. She gasped, her body trembling as she realized she'd fallen apart in front of her bosses and the sheriff of Slick Rock. She felt the slide of the comforter beneath her body, realizing she was totally naked and covered in a large, heavy blanket. She pushed the blanket aside, heading into the bathroom. She definitely needed a shower. Although her body felt lethargic, her mind and heart felt peaceful for the first time in years.

Felicity stepped into the shower, scrubbed her hair and body, and then let the shower spray over her aching body. The hot water did wonders for her muscles, making her reluctant to get out. She leaned her head against the cool tile wall, relishing the warm water easing her pains. She didn't hear the bathroom door open, but when she felt a cool gust of air, she opened her eyes to see Tom and Billy watching her through the open glass door of the shower.

"Are you all right, sweetheart?" Tom asked, scrutinizing her face.

Felicity smiled, nodded her head, and then turned the taps off. She stepped down out of the shower, and Billy pulled a clean towel from the countertop, enveloping her within its warmth. Tom grabbed another clean towel then began to rub her hair dry. She had never felt so pampered in her life. She closed her eyes with a sigh of contentment and leaned back into Billy. When they had finished drying her, Billy left the bathroom and was back in moments with some of her clean clothes. He helped her dress then stepped back as Tom picked up a comb and began to untangle her long black hair. He didn't hurt her once. He began at the bottom of her hair and worked his way up to her scalp. Once done, they left Felicity to brush her teeth with the suggestion she join them in the kitchen when she was done.

Felicity sat down in the kitchen a few seats away from Tom and Billy. They surprised her when they rose to their feet and moved to sit on either side of her. Nanette bustled around the kitchen with the last preparations for lunch, just before the ranch hands began to wander into the room. They each smiled and nodded at her then got down to the business of eating. Felicity kept to herself until they all headed back outside to work again.

"I need you to talk, Flick. You scared the hell out of us last night. Please, tell us why you were so upset. The last thing we want is to scare you, or have you make yourself sick," Tom said earnestly.

"Can we talk about this later? Please?" Felicity asked as she glanced toward Nan.

"Sure, baby. Whatever you want," Billy replied.

"I guess I should get back to work," Felicity said with a sigh. The last thing she felt like was working, but she knew that's what she had been hired to do.

"Felicity, I want you come into the study. Please?" Tom asked, rising to his feet, holding a hand toward her.

Felicity didn't hesitate to take Tom's hand. She knew they weren't going to let her get away without explaining, so she resigned herself to following her boss.

* * * *

Tom led Felicity to the sofa in his office and pulled a chair from in front of his desk, straddling it so he could see her face. Billy followed suit, both of them waiting for her to speak.

"I'm sorry I scared you. I didn't mean to break down the way I did. When one of you called me Flick and accused me of lying, it brought back memories I had buried deep down in my heart. You see, my mom used to call me Flick. I remembered the way my mom used to sing to me when I was little, the scent of vanilla surrounding me as she cuddled me. I lost my parents when I was three years old and was sent to live with my elderly maiden aunt. Don't get me wrong, she took care of me, made sure I had clothes, food, and a roof over my head, but she never gave me what I truly needed. She never hugged me or gave me any love at all. I honestly don't know if she was capable of it. She taught me to clean and cook, so by the time I was nine years old, I was keeping house for her. She taught me to be self-sufficient. I didn't know until she died that she was a gambling addict. She never allowed me to have any friends over, or to visit anyone, so eventually I began to push people away. It was just easier, you know. Not to have to make excuses all the time. I didn't feel like a whole human being. I used my work to keep me going. My aunt died when I was seventeen years old, and since I had no friends, I think I compensated by wanting to be close to animals. I felt needed for the first time in my life. I kept my distance from people, worked as much as I could to keep the loneliness at bay. I was a human automaton, not feeling, just going through the process of existing."

"I'm sorry we made you feel bad, sweetheart," Tom said. "That was never our intention. If you want to leave, we'll let you go, but don't think we don't want you here, because we do. We want you a whole damn lot. Now, regarding work. You're not to work for at least two weeks. Doc's orders. We had Doc come out last night. He gave you a sedative shot, to calm you down. He thought you were on the edge of a nervous breakdown. Since we are your employers, it is our duty to see that you're well. You will not be helping out for at least two weeks. The only time I want to see you in that yard is to get some fresh air or go for a ride. You are to get others to tack up for you, no heavy lifting. One of us will be with you at all times. We want to take care of you, Felicity. Do you understand?"

"Yeah, I think so. Can I ask you both a question?"

"Sure, baby. Shoot," Billy replied.

"Why are you two and the sheriff trying to get me into bed?"

"We like you a lot, sweetheart. Billy and I have always liked to share women. I can't tell you why, really. It's just that we seem to have a connection when we love a woman. We both always seem to like the same women. When we were younger, we used to fight all the time over women. Trying to steal from the other. One day the woman we were fighting over suggested we have a threesome. We enjoyed it so much we haven't looked back since. We seem to feed off of each other's excitement. We've been looking to settle down with a woman we can both share. Someone we want to spend the rest of our lives with, have kids, and grow old with. We both think you may be that woman," Tom explained.

"Oh my God. You really want to share me? All the time? That's why you were all in my bedroom? I thought you were just trying to seduce me to have sex with all three of you, not for a permanent relationship."

"Yeah, baby," Billy replied. "Take all the time you need, sweetheart. Take those two weeks to heal and think about what you want. When, if you're ever ready, all you have to do is come to us. Let us know what you want. We'd never hurt you. The last thing we want to do is hurt you. We want to give you pleasure. We want to love you."

"I've never heard of anything like this happening in real life. I've read about it, but I don't know if I can do this! You need to give me some time to think things through. Where does Luke come into this? He was in my bedroom as well."

"We have been friends with Luke since we were kids. He took one look at you and wanted you as well. I think if it had been anyone else, we would have punched their lights out, but we couldn't do that to a friend," Tom explained.

"How can you want me? You don't even know me! I don't know you. Oh God, I just don't know."

"We know we turn you on, sweetheart. We've seen it in your eyes. Please, don't say no until you give it, us, a chance. We won't do anything unless you want us to, but please, just don't say no," Tom reiterated.

"I'm so confused. I don't know what to think."

Felicity sat staring at them. She had no idea whether she could do what they were asking of her. She'd never even been with one man, let alone three! She watched as the two men stood, moved to her, giving her a kiss on her head, and then they left the room without a backward glance. Felicity had no idea how long she sat staring into space, their words going around and around in her head. The thought of having three men stroke her body, sliding their hands over her skin, had her breathing rapidly, her nipples puckering into tight, hard nubs, and her pussy clenching, leaking cream onto her panties. She'd never had anyone really love her, besides her parents. The thought of having three men all to herself was very, very tempting.

Felicity lifted her head toward the doorway when she heard a shuffle of feet. She smiled when she saw Nan standing there with two cups of coffee in her hand.

"I thought you might like a cup of coffee and maybe a female to talk to. I know I'm not your mother, or even a female relation to you, but I already know what a sweet, loving person you are," Nanette said.

"I don't know what to do, Nanette. They want to share me. I'm so confused. How could they want to share me and be happy doing that? I can see so many problems with that scenario. I mean, what if one of them got jealous with the other and they began fighting? What if I accidentally spent more time with one and not the others? I just can't see it working."

"Have you asked them how it will work?"

"No, not yet. I was too flabbergasted to think. They totally blew me away when they told me what they wanted."

"I've been working on this ranch for the last eight years. I've seen women come and go, and yes, they shared those women. I have never seen them look at the other women the way they look at you. You need to tell them about your concerns. You need to be comfortable with what they want from you. If you're not comfortable, then I can't see it working. But out of all of this, there needs to be love. No relationship can work without love."

"What would people think about me if I decided to go ahead with what they want? I would be branded a loose woman, a slut. I don't know if the ranch hands would accept me anymore. Would they think I was available to any of them, if I do this? Oh God, Nanette. I'm so confused."

"The only person you need to answer to is yourself, Felicity. It doesn't matter what anyone else thinks. I know you love them all very much. I've seen it in your eyes. No, don't worry, I don't think those men have a clue. Are you willing to throw away your one and only chance of finding love and happiness? Or are you courageous enough to hold on with both hands and live your dreams? Think about it long and hard before you throw away what could be a once-in-a-lifetime chance. Find out how things will work if you decide to go ahead. But most importantly, follow your heart," Nanette advised. "Now, I'd best get back to the kitchen. If I don't have dinner ready in time, I'm going to have hungry bears on my hands."

"Thanks, Nanette. Thanks for listening and giving me your advice. I really appreciate it."

"Anytime, honey. Anytime."

Felicity sat in the study quietly pondering over Nanette's advice. She knew she couldn't lie to herself anymore. She wanted those three men more than she could stand. She could imagine what it would be like to have their hands and mouths on her body. She'd had a small taste, but it had been nowhere near enough to appease the raging hunger burning in her body. But she was scared to take the next step. Scared to give them everything she had only to have them throw it all away. She wondered what would be worse, having them and then losing them, or not having them at all. Then she thought about her parents, how they had lost their lives at such a young age. They had missed out on so much, and so had she. It was time to grab life with both hands and live every day as if it would be her last.

Chapter Eight

Luke found Felicity sitting quietly in the study when he got home from work. He could see the wheels turning in her head as expressions flitted across her face. She was concentrating so hard, she was unaware he was standing in the doorway. He moved further into the room then smiled as she turned her head to him.

"Hey, honey. How are you feeling?" Luke asked as he sat down on the sofa cushion beside her.

"I'm good. How was work?"

"Pretty quiet, which is just the way I like it," Luke replied with a grin. He just watched her curiously as she watched him. She turned her body toward him a little more, placed her small hand against his cheek, and gazed into his eyes.

"Do you have any idea how handsome you are? You're such a sexy man, Luke," Felicity stated quietly, her eyes looking at him with hunger.

"You're playing with fire, little girl," Luke whispered, his voice deeper than normal as his body heated with desire.

"Good," Felicity whispered as she leaned forward. "I can't wait to get burnt."

Luke moved quickly. He pulled her onto his lap and slammed his mouth down over hers. She didn't even have time to blink. He thrust his tongue between her lips, sweeping the interior of her mouth, sliding his tongue against hers in an erotic duel of carnality. He heard the breath rush out of her lungs. And then he was carrying her to the study door. He hesitated then drew his mouth from hers. He stopped when he saw movement off to the side and turned to look at the heated stares Tom and Billy were giving her. He heard her breath hitch and saw her lick her dry lips. The masculine groans that emanated from Tom and Billy had his cock jumping in his pants.

"Bedroom, now," Luke rasped. He took off down the long hallway, his long legs eating up the distance in no time. He didn't have to look back over his shoulder to see his friends following. He could practically feel their heated breath on his neck.

Luke gently put Felicity down on the mattress. Keeping his eyes on her, he began to strip the confining clothes from his body. He watched her as he revealed his body and knew she was as horny as he was. He could see it in her eyes. Her pupils were so dilated only small rings of her violet-blue irises could be seen. Her chest rose and fell rapidly as she panted for breath. Once he was naked, he crawled onto the bed, gathered her body against his own, and slammed his mouth down to hers. He groaned long and deep as his tongue thrust into her sweet, moist cavern, touching, tasting, exploring every inch of her mouth. He swept his hands down the sides of her body until he encountered the waistband of her jeans. He slid his hand from her hip, over her stomach, and pulled at the button holding her jeans together. He used one of his arms, sliding it beneath her hips to lift her ass, slid the zipper on her pants down, and tugged.

Luke felt the bed dip and knew Tom and Billy had just joined them on the bed. He opened his eyes, still keeping his mouth on Felicity's, and gave a groan of relief as his two friends helped to strip their woman. She was naked from the waist down in moments. He slowly weaned his mouth from Felicity's, licking and nibbling his way across her face, along the line of her jaw, licking around the rim of her ear, then down along her neck. He moved back to stare into her passion-glazed eyes, noting the pink hue coloring her cheeks. He watched as Tom gently turned her head to him to take her mouth.

Luke noticed Tom licking and nibbling along her lower lip, coaxing Felicity into responding to him. Luke's cock was so hard he was hurting. He wanted nothing more than to pick their woman up and slam her down on his hard, aching flesh. Instead he tried to temper his desire, not wanting to frighten Felicity away with his intensity. He tilted her head by grasping a handful of her hair, pushed his tongue into her mouth, dueling with her. He growled his approval when he felt her lips close around his tongue as she began to suckle on him. He could just imagine his hard cock in the place of his tongue. Need slammed into him, his control breaking. He slanted his mouth over hers, again and again. Tasting her desire on his tongue, taking her whimpers of need into his mouth. He couldn't get enough.

* * * *

Felicity was out of her mind with desire. Tom was now ravaging her mouth, thrusting his tongue in and out of her, mimicking the sex act. She didn't think she could stand much more. She wanted someone to relieve the heavy liquid ache in her lower belly. She needed her empty, clenching pussy to be filled. She didn't care who, but she needed to be fucked now.

"Oh God. Please," Felicity cried out. Her hips were arching off the bed, rocking in a steady rhythm, begging for someone to fill her cunt.

"Please what, sweetheart?" Tom panted out against her mouth.

"Someone fuck me. Please, I can't stand it anymore."

"Don't worry, honey. We'll take care of you," Luke replied. She saw him crawl to the end of the bed, and he gently spread her legs apart. He sat on his haunches, staring at the cream-covered lips of her sex. She wondered if he could see her cream pooling in her hole then slowly dribbling out down over her perineum and ass, tickling her sensitive flesh. Felicity saw Luke lean down over her pussy, breathe in her essence, open his mouth, and then he was there. He scooped his large hands beneath her ass and hips and tilted her up to lick her. The feel of his tongue licking from her puckered asshole to the top of her slit was so exquisite, she thought she'd died and gone to heaven. He licked her like she was a delicious ice cream, not wanting to lose a drop. Her eyes rolled back in her head, and she canted her hips up, begging for more. The feel of two other warm, wet mouths licking and biting over her breasts, as well as the tongue licking her slick, wet folds, was too much to bear.

Felicity's legs began to shake. Her stomach was quavering and aching. She felt like she was coiled so tight, she would snap. She screamed out loud, the walls of her pussy clamping and releasing, pleasure like she had never felt before wracking her entire body. She even felt her toes come. When she finally began to come back to herself, the sound of Luke growling as he licked up her juices had her body igniting once more. She opened her heavy eyelids to see three sexy men staring at her with such lust she nearly came again. Tom and Billy were on either side of her, each pumping his hand up and down his huge cock. She looked down her body to see Luke give her one last lick, and then he sat up between her legs. His chin was covered in her juices, and he was pumping his cock in his hand as he stared at her.

"I am going to fuck you so good, honey. When I'm done, Tom and Billy are going to fuck you, too," Luke rasped out. She kept her eyes on his as she felt him slide a finger into her tight pussy, rimming it around up to the first knuckle, coating his digit with her moisture. She whimpered as he slid his hand down between the cheeks of her ass, slowly massaging the bundle of nerves at her little pucker. He slid his finger back up to her pussy, gathering more of her cream, then back down to her bottom. She moaned as he slowly pushed his coated finger into her tight hole.

"Have you ever had anyone in your ass before, baby?" Billy asked. Felicity could see the fire glittering in his eyes as he watched what Luke was doing to her.

"No," Felicity whimpered, canting her hips to give Luke better access to her anus. She had no idea she had so many pleasurable nerve endings in her ass.

"Do you want to have a cock in your ass, sweetheart?" Tom asked as he pinched one of her nipples between his thumb and finger.

"I–I d–don't know?"

"Do you like what I'm doing to you, honey?" Luke asked, keeping his eyes glued to her face.

"Yes," Felicity moaned.

"Billy" was all Luke got out. Billy was off the bed then rummaging in the adjoining bathroom in seconds flat. He climbed back on the bed with something in his hand but hidden from view.

"Do you trust us, honey?" Luke asked with bated breath.

"Yes."

"Good. I'm going to stretch you now. You will feel a bit of a pinch and some burning, but you shouldn't feel any real pain. I want you to tell me if I hurt you, okay? The last thing I want to do is hurt you. You can tell me anytime to stop and I will," Luke reiterated.

"Okay."

"Good girl," Luke whispered.

Felicity watched Billy hand something over to Luke, but didn't quite see what. She heard a cap popping and closed her eyes, trepidation making her wary.

"A bit of cold, sweetheart," Tom crooned against her ear.

Felicity tried not to jump as the cold, wet finger touched her clenched asshole, but couldn't help it. Two sets of warm hands ran over her chest, kneading breasts, soothing her into relaxing her body. The feel of Luke's finger massaging her ass was so good she wanted more. She mewled low in her throat when she felt his finger begin to penetrate her tight hole. She could hear their crooning voices, but couldn't seem to pick up what they were saying. It didn't matter. She knew they were trying to soothe her. Felicity took a couple of deep breaths, commanding her muscles to relax. She felt a burning in her bottom hole and bit her lip to stop herself from protesting.

Luke's finger pushed into her anus, through the tight muscles, then wiggled around in her hole. She whimpered in protest as he withdrew his finger, but then he was back with more. He massaged her hole, spreading the lube onto her flesh, and then he was pushing into her ass once more. She did whimper this time. The burn and pinch was more potent than the last. She didn't know if she could take much more. She felt him push through her tight sphincter, pushing in her tight channel all the way. He slowly withdrew them from her body but not all the way. Then he was pushing them back in. He pumped his fingers in and out of her ass, a gentle glide and slide, then spread his fingers, stretching her virgin muscles. He repeated the process again, adding more lube, until he was pumping his fingers in and out of her ass quickly. Felicity cried out in protest when he withdrew his fingers completely.

"You are so fucking hot, honey. You just had three of my fingers up your ass. I can't wait to get my dick into that tight little hole," Luke stated in a gravelly voice.

Felicity couldn't answer. She was so hot and needy, she couldn't speak. She watched as Luke grasped her by her hips, flipped her over onto her stomach, and shoved a pillow beneath her hips. She heard the pop of the cap and knew Luke was going to fuck her ass. She would have been scared since she'd never done that before, but since he had taken time to prepare her, stretch her, she was totally fearless. Instead she tilted her hips, shoving her ass a little higher into the air. She felt Luke cover her body with his. He wrapped an arm around her waist as he whispered in her ear.

"Breathe in and out a few times for me, honey. Don't tense up, it will only hurt more. Try and keep your muscles as relaxed as possible."

Felicity felt the blunt, hard head of Luke's cock pushing against her ass. She tried to jerk away from the burning, pinching pain, but he held her fast. He pushed relentlessly until she felt the large corona of his cock pop through the tight ring of muscles. She panted in and out of her mouth, trying to breathe through the pain. She was grateful Luke held still, giving her virgin ass time to adjust to his penetration. Just as she began to relax, Luke pushed in another few inches. Having his penis forging its way into her ass felt so naughty and carnal she wanted more. Luke pulled out a little, and then he was pushing back in. He rocked his hips slow and steady until he was buried in her ass balls-deep. The pain was bearable, and she felt so full she couldn't stay motionless, but it still wasn't enough. Luke got up on his knees behind her, wrapped both his arms around her waist, and pulled her up onto his lap, his cock sliding a bit deeper into her ass. Felicity's ass was on fire. She couldn't stand it anymore.

"It hurts. Oh God, do something. Please," she cried, tears leaking from her eyes.

"Shh, it's okay, sweetheart. Just keep breathing deeply," Tom said, soothing her.

Felicity watched as Tom got up onto his knees, moved in close to Felicity, and plundered her mouth. He swirled his tongue around hers, bringing her pleasure back up to a slow burn. She felt him slide his fingers through the wet folds of her labia, stroking the tip of his finger around her engorged clit. Her legs began to quiver, and her lower belly jumped with every brush of his finger against her hard nub.

Felicity whimpered into Tom's mouth as he withdrew his finger from her clit. She felt the blunt end of his cock begin to push into her tight, wet sheath. She tried to push him away, and when he began to move away, she contradicted her actions by grabbing his hair and pulling him close to her. She had something she wanted to tell them, but Tom was kissing her so deeply she forgot what she wanted to say. She let herself relax, her muscles softening, accepting as Tom thrust into her pussy with one powerful surge.

Felicity winced with pain. Her insides felt as if they'd been split apart. She pushed against Tom's chest, tears flowing down her cheeks, her pussy clenching with the slight pain.

"That hurt you, Felicity. Why?" Tom asked.

"I was a virgin," Felicity replied shyly.

"Ah sweetheart, why didn't you tell me? I would have gone slower. Shh, easy, sweetheart. Don't move, Felicity. I'll make it better,

I promise," Tom stated.

She felt Tom move his hand down between their bodies. He massaged the pad of his finger over her clit, rubbing up and down, then in tight little circles. His shoulders seemed to slump in relief when she made mewling sounds, letting him know he had reignited her passion. She watched Billy move up to her from her side, and he took her mouth with his. He pulled back from her, got up on his feet until he stood on the mattress, and ran the head of his cock over her lips. She knew what Billy wanted, and she opened her mouth and sucked him down.

Felicity's first taste of Billy's cock in her mouth had her going wild. She began to rock her hips, trying to get the two men buried in her body to move. She whimpered with longing as she swirled her tongue over the head of Billy's rod then sucked him down to the back of her throat. She felt Tom pull out of her cunt until just the tip was resting in her hot, wet vagina. As Tom pushed back in, Luke pulled his cock out of her ass. Luke pushed back in, and Tom withdrew again. The two men in her ass and pussy set a slow, easy rhythm of glide and retreat, their cocks sliding over sensitive nerve endings in her tight canals. She bobbed her head up and down on Billy's cock, massaging the underside of his dick near the head with her tongue with every upward motion. In and out, they plundered, getting faster, harder, and deeper with every surge of their hips.

Felicity groaned around Billy's cock as her body began to tingle with warmth, shivers of pleasure racing up and down her spine, from the top of her head to the tips of her toes. She bobbed her head faster on Billy's hard flesh, up and down, until she felt him hitting the back of her throat. She moaned again, swallowing around his cock so she wouldn't choke on the pool of saliva in her mouth. Billy must have liked what she was doing, because he fisted a large hand in her hair and groaned.

"Fuck yeah, baby. Swallow on me again. Oh yeah, that's it, little girl. I love the way you look, my cock filling your mouth while you're getting fucked in your pussy and ass. Moan again, baby. Ah, so good. When I come, I'm gonna shoot down your throat and you're going to drink my cum."

Felicity couldn't believe Billy's dirty talk was turning her on so much. Her body was shaking and jerking. She could feel all the muscles in her body getting tight. Her pussy and ass muscles were rippling along the two cocks pumping in and out of her body. She began to keen in the back of her throat. The pleasure they were giving her was so good, too good, she didn't think she would be able to stand it. Her body was so taut she knew she was going to snap. And then she was there. Right at the top of the pinnacle, with only one way to go. Up and over. She screamed around Billy's cock, her body convulsing uncontrollably as her pelvic floor muscles clamped down on the two cocks in her ass and pussy. She felt Billy's cock throb, harden, and then he was drowning out her cries of ecstasy. He roared long and loud as he shot load after load of cum down her throat. Felicity was with Billy as they both raced toward the stars together. She was vaguely aware of Luke and Tom yelling out as they both reached their peaks, filling both her holes with copious amounts of cum. Dark spots were dancing before her eyes, and she thought she was about to pass out from too much pleasure. She slumped down onto Tom, knowing one of the men would catch her before she fell. She closed her eyes, her breath still billowing in and out of her lungs, her body slowly coming down from its climactic high.

Felicity whimpered with pain as Luke pulled his cock from her ass. Tom slowly withdrew from her pussy and gently lay her down on her side on the mattress. She thought about getting up and heading to the bathroom for a shower, but she just didn't have the energy. Her body was so heavy, sated beyond her dreams. She dozed lightly until she felt her men tending her.

She was only vaguely aware of lovers tending to her body, cleaning up the sticky residue of their lovemaking from between her thighs with warm, soapy washcloths. She heard the whispered curse and opened her eyes to slits and saw Tom looking at the blood mingling with his seed on the washcloth.

Chapter Nine

Felicity winced as she stretched out her sore, tired, aching muscles. She yawned, blinked a few times until her eyes would cooperate and stay open. Sunlight was streaming through her bedroom window, making it hard for her eyes to adjust to the brightness. She flung the covers off, swung her legs over the side of the bed, stood up, and headed to the bathroom. Once showered and dressed, she opened the bathroom door and found three sets of eyes staring at her intensely. She hesitated in the doorway, wondering what was going on. Usually Luke headed to work as soon as breakfast was over, and it was a lot later in the morning than breakfast time.

"Come here, honey," Luke requested, holding a hand out toward her.

Felicity took a deep breath, let it out slowly, and walked over to Luke. Once her hand was in his, he pulled her to the bed and sat down with her at his side, not relinquishing his hold on her.

"Why didn't you tell us you were a virgin, sweetheart? I know I hurt you, and that's the last thing I wanted. If you'd told us we would have gone a lot easier on you," Tom stated.

Felicity felt her cheeks becoming red and lowered her eyes. She didn't know if he was upset with her or himself but really didn't want to know.

"I tried, but you didn't listen. I tried to push you away before, before, you know...but you kissed me, and then it was too late."

"Fuck it, Flick. You should have tried harder," Billy stated.

Felicity's anger began to build. They had no right to be angry with her. She hadn't done anything wrong. She pulled away from Luke and stood, her arms crossing her chest defensively. "I don't know what you're all so fucking angry about. It's my body that's tender, not yours."

"Watch your mouth, honey. I don't like to hear our woman cussing," Luke commanded, his eyes narrow slits.

"Well, who the hell made you my keeper? I am not a child and won't be treated like one. So you three can just go and, go and, fuck off," Felicity yelled then spun around and took off. She needed a moment to herself to cool off before she said something she would regret. Ten minutes later, she entered the room and looked up at Luke.

"I'm sorry for being such a bitch. I don't know why I acted like that."

Luke pulled her close and cuddled her. He placed his hand over hers, silently asking permission to remove her towel. Felicity let go, and he removed the towel from around her body. She had forgotten about her little surprise. She'd shaved her pussy in the shower and had been saving it as a surprise. They had just ruined it.

She found herself lying naked on the bed, her limbs tied spread-eagle with the soft restraints they'd used the other night. She was in for it now, and she couldn't wait for her punishment to begin.

"You will not speak another cuss word, or we will punish you every time you do. One of us will put you over our knees and spank your ass until it's a pretty pink color. Do you understand, Felicity?" Tom asked, crossing his arms over his chest waiting for a reply.

Felicity's pussy clenched at the thought of being spanked. What was up with that? She shouldn't be getting horny being teased with a spanking. She closed her eyes, refusing to answer. Who the hell did they think they were? What right did they have to tell her what she should and shouldn't do?

"Billy, go get the stuff we need, oh, and the baby oil," Luke commanded, standing over Felicity.

Felicity knew Tom was watching her quiet defiance. But she could see he and his brother and friend were determined to get what they wanted by the steely glint in his eyes.

Felicity felt trepidation shiver up and down her spine. She knew Tom and Luke were staring at her, making her feel vulnerable being spread out before them in all her naked glory. She could hear Billy rummaging around in the adjoining bathroom and was curious about what he was doing, but more than determined to keep her eyes closed. She heard water running from the bathroom faucet and tried to open her eyes to slits, peering beneath her eyelashes to see what was going on. Since her eyes weren't fully open, she could just make out the outline of Tom and Luke standing off to her side. She slammed her eyes shut when she heard Billy entering the room once more.

Felicity gasped when she felt one of the men took a hold of her hips, and she was flipped over onto her stomach. One of them shoved a couple of pillows beneath her hips, and then they ran soothing hand over the skin of her ass. She moaned at the wonderful sensation of those hands caressing her flesh. Then she was held down by two sets of hands. Her hips were held up slightly, and the third set of hands began to knead the soft, fleshy globes of her butt. The hands on her hips let go, and then she felt a stinging slap land on one cheek. She screeched and turned her head to see who had spanked her. Felicity opened her eyes, preparing to give them all a mouthful, but their heated gazes prevented her from speaking. Her chest tightened with desire, suspending her venomous tirade.

She couldn't believe how turned on they were by giving her a spanking. She let her head flop down onto the bed again and yelled as another sharp slap landed on her ass. The hand delivering her punishment rubbed over her heated flesh, and she couldn't stop the moan from erupting from her throat. It seemed as if they weren't the only ones getting turned on. The warmth from the whacks she was enduring was travelling down to her pussy, making her clit tingle and her cunt pulse. Another smack landed and another. No two whacks to her ass were ever in the same spot. She became aware of the fact she was pushing her hips up practically begging for the next blow. She could feel cream dripping from her pussy, and she was coiled so tightly, she knew another few smacks to her ass would send her into climax. She felt her cunt clench and release, begging to be filled, to release her from her unrequited desire.

She turned her head again in time to see Tom pick up a bottle of flavored oil. He poured a little of the oil into the palm of his hand then rubbed his hands together, warming it and coating his palms and fingers. He then began to massage his hands into the heated skin of her ass and underneath to her bare mound. She couldn't prevent the moan emitting from her throat as she tried to buck her hips up into his massaging fingers. They flipped her back over onto her back and Tom massaged more oil into her nude pussy.

"Oh yeah. You like that, don't ya, baby? It feels so much more sensitive now that your pubes are gone, doesn't it? I can't wait to get my mouth on that pretty little cunt. I can just imagine sucking those plump little lips into my mouth, sucking on your cute little clit." Billy smacked his lips together in anticipation of his delectable meal.

Felicity felt Tom spread her labia apart then slide his fingers up and down her slit, spreading her cream up to her clit. He used the pad of one of his fingers, massaging her clit with light butterfly circles. He swirled his finger around and around her little nub, the circles getting closer and closer to her most sensitive spot.

"You like that, don't you, sweetheart? I can't wait to get my mouth on your little erection. You have no idea how much it turns us on to see you like this. Your face is pink with need, your breasts jiggling with every breath you take. I could lie between your sleek thighs and eat you for hours on end. Oh, you like that idea. I saw your pretty little cunt open and close, just begging to be filled."

Felicity watched Tom as he removed his hand from her pussy. He once again retrieved the bottle of flavored oil, tilted the bottle, pouring some more liquid into the palm of his hand. He dipped two fingers into the oil pooling in his cupped hand, coating his digits liberally. He leaned down to her pussy and blew his warm, moist breath over her clit. She bucked her hips up, mewling in the back of her throat, her eyes closing at the pleasure he bestowed on her. The feel of a warm, wet tongue flicking over her clit had her crying out loud for more.

Felicity's breath was now rasping in and out of her lungs at a rapid pace, and her pussy was dripping her juices out from her hole, which dribbled down to coat her ass then onto the sheet below her. She cried out again as Tom sucked her distended clit into his mouth, between his lips, suckling her sensitive flesh. She thrust her hips up, cried out loud, then sobbed out her pleasure as Tom's oil-coated fingers thrust into her tender cunt. Two warm, wet mouths descended onto her hard nipples, sucking, biting, and laving the turgid peaks. She could feel liquid warmth pooling in her lower abdomen and knew she was close to climaxing.

* * * *

Tom felt Felicity's cunt walls ripple along the length of his fingers. He knew she was getting close to orgasm. He twisted his fingers in her pussy until his palm was facing up and curled his fingers inside her, searching out her sweet spot. He slid his fingers in and out of her body, making a "come here" motion, all the while licking and sucking on her clit. He could feel her muscles tightening around his digits, preparing to send her over the edge into ecstasy. He picked up the pace of his pumping fingers, making sure to give a little tug as he pleasured her. The liquid slurping sounds of her pussy had his cock jerking in his pants as she rose closer and closer to release. He sucked her clit into his mouth, gently holding the sensitive bundle of nerves between his teeth, spread his tongue out until it was flat, and licked her like he was a man dying of thirst. Then she was there, right on the edge. His little woman screamed, her body bowing off the bed, her pussy walls clamping down onto his fingers so hard he wondered if he would ever be able to pull them out of her body. He curled his fingers, rubbing the pads of them over her rough G-spot, enhancing her pleasure to the ultimate experience a woman could achieve. She screamed as her pussy expelled her cum from her body in a long stream then a copious gush of milky fluid and the sound of her keening made him want to shove his cock into her clenching sheath and ride her until he reached his own release. Her fluids dripped down over his hand, shot out onto his thighs, onto his chin, and into his mouth. He growled his approval, the taste of her sweet release coating his tongue, his fingers still massaging her G-spot. Her body was twitching and shaking uncontrollably, her cries of release loud, echoing through the room. Tom was beyond control. Now that he'd had a taste of her juices, he wanted more.

Tom didn't give their woman time to come back down from her climactic high. Instead he kept his fingers pumping and massaging over her erogenous zone. He released her clitoris from his mouth, began lapping at her flesh again and again. He licked up all her sweet juices, not wanting to waste a drop of her cum, then flicked his tongue over her engorged little nub rapidly. He lifted his eyelids to watch his brother and best friend sucking on Felicity's nipples and running their hands over her upper torso. The sight of Felicity's head thrashing back and forth on the pillow beneath her head, her chest and face covered with a pink hue, was one of the most beautiful sights he had ever seen. He lowered his lashes once more, concentrating on sending their woman into orbit again.

Tom was surprised when he felt Felicity's vaginal walls flutter around his fingers once more. He thought it would take her longer to reach her peak since she'd only just come. He upped the pace of his thrusting, massaging fingers within her tight, wet cunt, flicking his tongue over her blood-engorged clit. He growled in his throat when he felt her internal muscles tightening around his fingers and knew she was on the edge once more. He hooked his fingers again, making sure to slide the pads of his digits over her G-spot, then sucked her clit into his mouth firmly. Felicity's scream of pleasure had his cock throbbing, a tingling warmth spreading from the base of his spine, down to his tight balls, then up his rigid cock. He groaned around her clit as she drenched him with her milky, white cum as it expelled from her body, and he shot his own load into his tight boxers. He slowed his pumping fingers as the clench and release of Felicity's inner muscles fluttered one last time then stopped. He withdrew his dripping digits from her cunt, shoved them into his mouth, and licked them clean. His woman's body was still twitching intermittently, but her eyes were closed and her body was lax with satiation. He grimaced when he moved, sticky cum pulling at his pubic hair, coating his underwear.

"Shit, Tom. You made our little girl pass out," Luke said with a grin.

"Yeah, she's something, isn't she? I've never known such a responsive woman," Tom stated as he smoothed his hands up and down Felicity's thighs.

"I was so turned on by her slurping pussy and the sounds coming from my mouth, I nearly came in my pants," Billy stated, grabbing his crotch.

"I did," Tom replied with a big smile then burst out laughing, his brother and friend joining in, guffawing loudly.

"I'll go fill the tub so we can clean our little honey up. Billy, when we have her in the tub you can strip and remake the bed," Luke said with a smile.

"Our little baby sure knows how to come hard, don't she?" Billy said lasciviously, wiggling his eyebrows as he grinned.

"That she does, little brother. That she does."

* * * *

Felicity awoke and found herself surrounded by hot, hard male bodies. She glanced to her left, right, then down to the end of the bed. Luke was on one side of her, and Billy was on the other. Tom was lying at the foot of the bed sideways, a pillow beneath his head, one of his hands on her calf. She eased her way from between the big men and climbed over the side of the bed, heading for the bathroom. She took care of her needs, dressed, and entered the bedroom again. The sight of Billy and Luke cuddling one another had her covering her mouth to stifle the giggles threatening to erupt. The noise must have been enough to wake her men, because all three opened their eyes. She couldn't hold in her amusement any longer. She burst out laughing, tears rolling down her cheeks. She doubled over clutching her stomach when Luke and Billy jumped away from each other, the expressions of surprise then distaste crossing their faces adding to her mirth. She ended up down on her knees laughing so much she could hardly breathe. The two men eying her with grimaces slowly let their amusement show.

"You think that's funny, do ya, baby? Next time you get out of bed before us, wake us up," Billy said, his beginning grin tilting the corners of his mouth. She saw Billy look from her to Tom and Luke, then back to her again. Her laughter must have been contagious, and before she knew it, they were all laughing along with her. It took a while, but finally they all settled down.

"You looked so sweet and cute cuddled up together," Felicity stated, another giggle erupting from her.

"Yeah, yeah. All right, the show's over. Let's go get some food. I don't like the fact that you've missed dinner two nights in a row, honey. You need to keep your strength up. From now on, you'll be eating three meals a day," Luke specified firmly.

"Oh good. I'm starving," Felicity stated, turned on her heels and left, putting an enticing sway in her hips that had the three men groaning. She looked back over her shoulder and saw them all adjusting their cocks. She was finally back in the land of the living and intended to enjoy every moment.

Chapter Ten

Felicity was enjoying life for the first time. She went horse riding and walking, read, and relaxed. She had never felt so alive. She made sure to rest every afternoon, even though she felt fine. She took the opportunity to catch up on her reading. She would sit out on the back veranda every afternoon, read until her eyelids began to droop, and then she would take a nap on the long bench seat swing. She was usually awoken by one of her men kissing her until she stirred. She was eating three meals a day and was gaining the weight she should have been carrying on her slender frame. She was no longer skin and bones. She had a healthy glow to her, and her muscles were more pronounced from riding every morning. Her three men were loving her every night, and then they would cuddle up with her after they had bathed her. Life couldn't have been much better. She was at the end of her forced sabbatical with only two days left before she would return to work as a ranch hand. She didn't really want to return to work. She was quite happy and content being a lady of leisure, now that she'd had a taste, but knew it wouldn't be fair to Tom and Billy. She would feel guilty not helping out.

Felicity felt her eyelids drooping and knew, as much as she wanted to keep reading, her body wouldn't allow it. She picked the book up, and got up to go inside. She made her way into the living room, lay down on the sofa, and dozed. She was still aware of the sounds of cattle and horses drifting in through the open windows and screen door as her mind drifted in that place between sleep and wakefulness. She heard the sounds of boots on the veranda steps and then the screen door opened, but she couldn't open her eyes to see which one of her men was heading toward her. She just continued to drift. She felt whoever it was stop next to her and smiled, letting them know she was aware they were near. The hand that covered her mouth firmly had her jerking and her eyes snapping open. She looked up into the angry gaze of James. She tried to sit up, but he placed a hand on her chest, holding her down with painful pressure. She reached out with her arms, trying to pry his hands off her mouth and chest. She scratched down his arm, satisfied she had hurt the bastard when he cursed. She didn't see the fist coming until it was right in her face. Pain exploded in her jaw, shooting into her head and down her neck. She saw stars then slumped into the beckoning darkness.

* * * *

Felicity groaned, pain radiating from her jaw to her pounding head. She opened her eyes only to close them again, light from a bare lightbulb making her flinch in pain. She opened her eyes again, taking in her surroundings. She had no idea where she was, but she knew she was no longer at the ranch. It looked like she was in a small hut. The walls were made from weathered timber, the roof from corroded tin. She looked down to find herself on a crude version of a bed, a fire burning brightly in a hearth. Her hands and legs were bound together with abrasive rope that cut into the skin of her wrists and ankles. The small hut was empty, and she knew she was in deep trouble. She couldn't believe James had hit her then kidnapped her. He obviously had a screw or two loose.

Felicity tried to wiggle her hands out of the ropes holding her arms behind her back, but only managed to scrape her wrists raw. She could feel the warmth of blood trickling over her wrists and gave up trying to get free. She hoped James didn't come back anytime soon. She wanted to try and escape before he arrived. She used her stomach muscles, pulling herself into a sitting position, then swung her bound legs off the side of the bed. She jumped over to the door of the cabin, turned her back to the door, stood up on her toes, and fumbled around for the doorknob. She turned the knob with her fingers, jumped back around and then out the door, using her shoulders to push the door open.

She took in her surroundings and knew she was going to have to find a place to hide. She could see a copse of trees in the distance and knew they were her only chance of hiding. She began the tedious, arduous task of jumping toward her destination. It seemed to take her hours to jump no more than a hundred yards. The muscles in her legs were burning with fatigue, lactic acid making her limbs feel heavy.

The sky was changing to pinks and purples, the sun was setting, and she knew she was running out of time. She had no idea how long she had been in the small hut, but she knew it didn't really matter. She hoped Luke, Tom, and Billy knew she was missing, knowing they were her only hope of escape from the deranged ex-ranch hand. She pushed the pain of her burning calves and thighs to the back of her mind, picking up the pace of her jumping motion. She needed to get to those trees.

She paused her movements as she heard the motor of a vehicle in the distance. Her time had just run out. She sobbed but took off jumping as quickly as she could, hoping she hadn't wasted any precious time by listening to the approaching vehicle. The sun was nearly gone from the sky, twilight lengthening shadows along the dry, long grass she was moving through. She caught the glare of headlights and quickly ducked down into the tall grass, not daring to move, not wanting to give her position away to whoever was out there, just in case it was James returning to the hut. She heard the vehicle stop, the engine no longer running. She held her breath and shivered uncontrollably when the sound of a male's voice echoed over the field. The sound of pure and utter rage permeated the air, making goose bumps cover her cold skin. She was so scared her heart was racing and she was panting in and out through her mouth. She exhaled quietly as she heard the sound of the vehicle start, the wheels of the four-wheel-drive, dual-cab utility spinning on the grass. She wanted to get up and bolt, but knew it would be absolutely futile. She stayed hidden in the grass as the vehicle sped across the open field. She exhaled again as the vehicle headed away from her. She rose up on her haunches slightly, trying to see where James was heading, but quickly ducked down again as the vehicle turned. She held her breath as the vehicle headed in her direction. He was obviously using his headlights to search for her. He sped past her, only yards separating her from the wheels of his truck. Fear making her body shiver and shake. She heard the truck turn once more, the sound of the engine much closer to her hiding place than the last time. She kept her eyes wide open, preparing to roll away from the deadly tires of the truck. She flattened herself out, rolled, and cursed as the car rolled to a stop over the top of her body. She bit her lip to contain her cry of pain, as the undercarriage of the truck struck her knee just before she flattened out. She was in danger of vomiting. Pain was shooting from her knee up and down her leg. She could taste blood in her mouth, dribbling down her chin from the cut in her lip from her teeth. She didn't dare release her lip, knowing if she did she would cry out in agony. The pain finally eased, giving way to a dull, persistent, burning throb. She opened her eyes wide, hearing the car door open, watching as booted feet landed on the ground so close to her. She breathed quietly in and out of her nose, hoping he wouldn't hear her, closed her eyes, and prayed.

"I will find you, you fucking bitch," James yelled hysterically. "Don't think you've won. I'm not leaving until I have you. I am going to fuck you so hard. It's your fault those bastards sacked me. I am going to make you pay. I will use your body over and over again. When I'm done with you, I am going to kill you. It won't be quick either. I am going to slice you up into little pieces, then leave what's left of your body for animals to pick over."

Felicity closed her eyes as she listened to James rave, his voice screaming out what he intended to do to her. She could see his feet moving from side to side in agitation and knew he was definitely insane. She hoped now he had driven over her hiding place, he would move to another area of the field. She was going to have to stay where she was. There was no way in hell she could move again. She was in way too much pain, and God knows what damage had been done to her right knee.

Felicity listened as James's ranting stopped, and then he cursed under his breath, got back into the car, and drove off. She stayed where she was, not daring to move, but listening intently as his vehicle roamed the open field searching for her. Her knee was throbbing like a bitch, her body shivering with cold even though she knew it wasn't that cold at all. She was in shock. She hoped like hell her men would turn up and find her soon. She was beginning to feel quite ill, knowing if she didn't get warm soon, she could be in real trouble.

Chapter Eleven

Luke arrived home from work, anticipating loving their woman after dinner making his cock hard. He stomped up the veranda steps hoping to find Felicity napping on the swing seat. He entered the house and saw her book on the floor in the living room, thinking it was unusual for her to leave her books lying around. He picked up the book and perused the cover, a big grin crossing his face when he saw the picture of one female and three men. The cover was very erotic, the vision making his cock jump in his pants. Taking the book with him, he headed to the kitchen to greet Felicity with a passionate kiss.

Luke entered the kitchen, breathing deeply as the aroma of the food Nan was cooking for dinner enticed his nostrils.

"Hey, Nan, something smells good."

"I'll bet you're nice and hungry, too, after a long day of keeping law and order. Dinner should be ready in about half an hour. Why don't you get cleaned up and bring that little girl in off the swing. She's probably thirsty after spending all afternoon out in the fresh air," Nan said.

"She's not inside?" Luke asked with a frown.

"Not that I know of, usually I hear her come in. Why?"

"I found her book on the floor in the living room, so she had to have come inside. I thought she must have dropped it without noticing before she went to the bedroom."

"That's not like our girl. She's always so careful of her books," Nan stated.

"Yeah, I know. I have a sinking feeling in my gut, Nan. I think I'll wander over to the barn and see if she's in there with Tom or Billy,"

Luke shouted over his shoulder, hurrying out of the house.

"Let me know if you find her," Nan called. Luke gave Nan a wave as he headed to the barn to let her know he'd heard her. He was in a hurry to find his woman.

Luke walked into the doorway of the barn, let his eyes adjust from the bright sunlight to the dim interior of the building, and called for his friends and lover.

"Tom, Billy, Felicity, are you in here?" he called as he moved further into the building.

"Here," Tom called then appeared from the tack room. "What's up?"

"Have you seen Flick?"

"She's on the swing on the veranda," Tom answered.

"No, she's not. She's not in the house either. Where's Billy?"

"He was in the loft last time I heard," Tom said, pointing to the ladder leading to the loft of the barn, then called loudly for his brother.

"What?" he yelled back then hung his head over the edge of the loft floor.

"Have you seen Flick?" asked Luke.

"Veranda swing," Billy stated.

"Fuck it. I knew something was wrong when I couldn't find her in the house. We need to search for her. I've had a sinking feeling in my gut ever since I found her book on the floor in the living room," Luke stated. "Where could she have gone?"

"None of the horses are missing. Maybe she's gone for a walk," Billy suggested.

"When was the last time you've seen our girl leave her precious books lying around on the floor?" Luke asked.

"Never," Billy replied.

Dread made Luke's heart sink to his stomach.

He looked from Tom to Billy and back again, agitation making him shift restlessly as he thought about where their lover could have gone. He hit on the same conclusion as his friends when their voices of fury joined his.

"James."

* * * *

Felicity's teeth were chattering in her mouth, her body shivering uncontrollably. Her head was pounding, her jaw and knee throbbing. She could feel bile rising up in her throat and knew she was going to be ill, but was thankful she couldn't hear James's car roaring through the open field anymore. She hoped he had given up searching for her and was long gone. Her arms and shoulders were aching from being restrained at an unnatural angle behind her back. Her fingers were freezing cold and totally numb. Her wrists were raw and sore, and she could just feel a small stream of blood trickling down her flesh. Her feet and toes had gone totally numb, and her legs were throbbing because of lack of circulation. In other words, she was a total mess. She'd tried countless times to get her body to cooperate, to push herself into a sitting position, but her arms were aching so much and her fingers were so numb, she knew it was a useless endeavor. But she refused to give up. After each attempt, she would rest her tired, aching body until she felt a little of her waning strength return. She couldn't allow that bastard to win. Not when she'd finally found a reason to live, to enjoy life to the fullest. She was so in love with her three lovers and vowed they would know how she felt. She wanted to spend the rest of her life loving the men she had only just found. She wanted to have their children, share the sorrows and joys life threw their way until they grew old. She wasn't giving up without a fight.

Renewed energy flowed through her body, giving her the determination she needed to bear the pain she knew was coming. She took a deep, fortifying breath, letting it out slowly, and rolled to her stomach. She gritted her teeth together, using her aching shoulders to steady her upper torso, and bent her knees. She pushed the pain shooting from her right knee to the back of her mind and pushed up with all her might. The guttural growl emanating from her throat sounded like a wounded animal, but she panted through the agony. With one last breath and her remaining strength, she jumped to her feet. She stumbled, crying out, but remained on her feet by taking two little sideways jumps. She was standing, and that was all that mattered. She was going to make it back to her men if it took her all night.

* * * *

Jack saw Luke run to his car, pick up the microphone of his radio, and call his two deputies to get their asses out to the Double E Ranch pronto. While the sheriff was organizing his deputies and the equipment he wanted them to bring out to the ranch, Jack, Billy, and Tom were organizing the ranch hands to help search for the men's missing lover.

Jack, with help from Tom and the hands, tacked up the horses and made sure they had any emergency supplies they thought they would need. Nan was getting food and water ready for everyone, and Billy and Tom placed the small packs of food in their saddle bags.

By the time Jack, his bosses, and the ranch hands had secured the packs and bedrolls to the back of their saddles, Luke was greeting his two deputies. Luke had called his deputies in to drive the four-wheel drive behind the horses in case the vehicle was needed to get Felicity back to the house or to medical help. He knew his bosses weren't going to leave anything to chance. Luke handed out portable radios to him and the hands, mounted up beside Tom and Billy, and then they were off.

Jack had heard Luke tell Tom and Billy they weren't going to head back home until they had their woman safely back in their arms. His two bosses and the sheriff let their mounts have their heads as they raced across the open fields.

Jack directed the remaining hands to head in different directions, hoping they would cover more ground as they searched separately. He hoped his bosses and the sheriff were the ones to find Felicity before nightfall, but he didn't hold out much hope, since there was only about an hour of daylight left. He just hoped they got to her before that deranged bastard, James, could do any damage to the petite woman. Jack decided to head for the southernmost field near the old timber shack, which had been erected way before Tom and Billy had bought the Double E Ranch. The shack was a good place to bunk down in, if and when the weather turned bad in winter. All the ranch hands were aware of the shack, including ex-ranch hand James.

When Jack finally arrived near the shack, it had been dark for a couple of hours. His horse was breathing heavy and was sweating as Jack slowed him to a walk. He needed to cool his horse down slowly so he wouldn't catch a chill. He'd ridden his mount hard over the last couple of hours. Jack had wanted to slow walk so his animal wouldn't be so tired, but urgency kept them both moving. Jack stopped as he came to a section of tall grass that was flattened. He dismounted and hunkered down to peer at the ground. Something really heavy must have flattened the grass. He grabbed his flashlight from his saddle, flipped it on, lighting the flat grass. He could just make out tire tracks on the edge of the squashed grass. He quickly mounted, kneed his horse to a canter, and was sliding from his horse's back minutes later. The door to the small timber shack was wide open, and there were fire embers smoldering in the hearth. Jack went back outside, flipped his flashlight on once more, and began to study the ground near the shack. He could see where a heavy vehicle had been, but hoped to find a sign of a lighter person.

Jack worked his way out from the door, methodically studying the grass, following any sign of movement he could. He found a long, thin line of flat grass and knew he had found what he'd been searching for. The trail was leading toward the trees in the distance. He grabbed Caesar's reins and set off following the trail, pulling his stallion along behind him.

Jack froze in his tracks when Felicity's trail merged with that of the vehicle. He studied the area diligently, praying to God the loopy bastard hadn't run over his bosses' woman. He shone his torch in every direction, studying the ground as he moved, being careful not to wipe out any signs of life nearby. He squatted down onto his haunches when he spied a sizable dark blotch on the ground. He dipped two fingers into the thick liquid, hoping he was coating his fingers with oil, but his intuition was working really well, and he knew before he shone his light onto his fingers it was blood.

Jack studied the ground around him for a few minutes then expelled a breath of air as he saw the trail once again leading toward the trees. He took off at a jog, pulling Caesar behind him. He traveled maybe another hundred yards and dodged to the side so he wouldn't hurt the woman lying on the ground before him. He dropped his mount's reins, walked to the back of his saddle, and pulled out his first-aid kit and the portable radio he had stored in his saddlebags. He picked up the radio and called Luke as he felt Felicity's neck, sighing in relief when he felt a strong, steady pulse. Using his shoulder and chin to hold the portable radio to his ear and mouth, he untied the ropes around Felicity's wrists, moved her arms to a more natural angle, then moved to her feet to do the same. He grabbed the thermal blanket out of his first-aid kit and covered her in it, hoping to get some of her body temperature back.

"Luke, I've found her. She's alive but out cold. We're in the most southern field of Double E Ranch, near the old timber shack. She's pretty battered and bruised, and her arms and legs were tied with rope, but she'll be okay," Jack relayed.

"Thank God. We're no more than twenty minutes away, we'll be there as fast as we can. Don't move Felicity. I don't want her to suffer any more pain or damage than she already has. My deputies have already called for the paramedics. They should be able to drive along the gravel road near the trees. Access shouldn't be a problem this time of year. We're on our way. Thanks, Jack."

Jack dropped the portable radio to the ground and set about making sure Felicity was comfortable. He lifted the side of the thermal blanket, shining the light over the length of her body. Aside from having a swollen, bruised jaw and raw skin on her wrists and ankle from the rope, the only real damage he found was to her right knee. Her jeans were ripped at the knee, so he grasped the denim material of her jeans and ripped it away from her. Her knee was nearly twice its normal size. A large deep cut ran beneath her patella, blood seeping from the wound, and she was extremely cold to the touch. Jack placed the flashlight on the ground, facing up, knowing the others would see the stream of light shining up from the ground as they got closer to them. He lifted the thermal blanket, moved his large body in close to Felicity's back, wrapped his arms around her waist, and then settled the blanket back over her body. He knew the heat from his own body would help to warm her up faster. He also knew he loved Felicity like a sister. She had inveigled herself into his heart, and he knew he would do anything to keep her safe. He exhaled loudly, trying to control the raging fury at finding the small woman in such a state, but knew he was fighting a losing battle. The rage inside him was making his blood boil. He breathed in, held the breath, and then let it out slowly. He did this about ten times before the knot in his gut and his fury began to subside.

Chapter Twelve

Felicity could hear beeping sounds, but couldn't work out where they were coming from. She frowned knowing she had heard that noise before, but couldn't quite get her mind to tell her what the noise was. She licked her dry lips, trying to swallow, not quite managing the simple task. Her head was aching and her wrists were sore, but the pain in her knee was the worst of them all. She lifted a hand to her forehead, pushing her hair back away from her face, sighing with relief as the tickling sensations stopped. Someone took her hands in theirs and smoothed her hair back from her forehead again. She pried her sticky eyelids open to see her three men surrounding her, concern evident on their faces. She smiled at them, her eyes closing once more, too heavy to keep open. She was so tired and could feel herself beginning to drift off to sleep again. Just before she fell asleep, a cold ice block was rubbed across her lower lip, and she slid her tongue out, capturing the moisture. She felt her men kiss her tenderly. One placed a kiss on the forehead, and the other two on the back of her hands. She heard them speaking to her, but was too far gone to understand what they were saying. She drifted down to a deep sleep, breathing evenly as the numbing sensations pulled her back into unconsciousness.

* * * *

"God, she is so beautiful," Luke said as he kissed Felicity's forehead.

"Yeah, she is. I'm so glad she came to our ranch. I love her so much," Billy stated.

"We all do, Billy. She's absolutely perfect for us. We are gonna have to hire another ranch hand. There is no way in hell I'm having our woman busting her gut every day on the ranch. Do you think she'd marry us? Make a life and babies with us?" Tom asked uncertainly as he looked over at Luke.

"There is only one way to find out, my friends. We are going to have to tell her how we feel and then ask her to marry us. There is no way in hell I'm letting her out of my sight for the next month. I've put in for some leave owing to me and it's been accepted. The county is sending another sheriff to fill in and maybe stay here permanently. Apparently this guy is an ex-Marine. He's not long out of the Special Forces. He's served quite a few years in the Middle East, but now that his time's done, he's looking for a quieter life," Luke said.

"Can't say I blame him. We'll have to invite him out to the ranch for a meal. Let him take in the simplicity of country life, maybe go for a ride. It's the least we can do after the way he's heroically fought in a war, protecting our country. Do you know what his name is?" Tom asked.

"Nope. Apparently he's still in debriefing for his job. The government isn't letting anything out of the bag until he's totally free of the services. I guess I'll find out tomorrow. He's supposed to arrive tomorrow night or early Tuesday morning. Apparently he has two brothers who are moving here as well. One of his brothers served with him and the other was a military mechanic," Luke stated.

"You know a fair bit of information, considering no names have been released yet. Do you know what the brothers are going to do with their lives?" Billy asked.

"Well, the mechanic is hell-bent on opening a mechanic shop, and the youngest wants to open up and run his own bar."

"Well, things are beginning to look up for Slick Rock. We only have the old hotel that's about to fall down around the owner's ears, and old Sly MacGregor has had an unfair advantage of being the only mechanic in town. It's about time there was a little competition around here. I'd love to be a fly on the wall when Sly finds out about the new mechanic and his shop. I can see the steam coming out of his ears now." Tom chuckled.

"It will definitely be interesting," Luke replied with a grin then looked back down to Felicity. She looked so small and fragile lying unconscious in the hospital bed with tubes and monitors all over her.

"It certainly will," Billy added.

* * * *

Felicity was happy to be back home on the Double E Ranch. She was lucky to have only suffered a mild case of hypothermia due to shock, bruising to her jaw, and abrasions on her wrists and ankles, as well as a deep cut, which had required quite a few stitches, beneath her knee. She had been lying on the sofa in the living room for the past five days, convalescing after her horrifying ordeal with James.

Luke and his two deputies had found James wandering the streets of Slick Rock, and now he was safely ensconced in a psychiatric ward in the large hospital in Denver, Colorado. She had been home for just under a week now and was looking forward to getting her stitches removed from her knee. She had an appointment to see Doc to have them removed in a couple of hours. Her injury site was totally healed, but the stitches were driving her mad. They itched like the devil.

Felicity's men hadn't touched her intimately since she been home from the hospital, and she was beginning to think they didn't want her sexually anymore. She'd set plans in motion to seduce her men after dinner and could hardly sit still, anticipation of the evening ahead having her in two minds. She was afraid they didn't want her, but she needed to find out. She was so in love with the three men, and she knew if they didn't reciprocate her feelings she was going to have to leave.

All of her men had been driving her crazy, checking on her every half an hour to an hour. The first day they she arrived home, they hadn't left her alone for a second. They were still very overprotective, but Luke was the worst of them all. He was on a month's leave, and even though he wasn't spending every waking moment with her now, he was still checking on her every half hour.

Felicity was becoming downright bitchy, but couldn't seem to control her irritable behavior. She'd never been one to snap and snarl for no reason and knew she wasn't being her normal, cool, emotionless self. She was putting her moods down to sexual frustration, as well as cabin fever. She had been a lot happier and freer with her emotions since coming to live on the Double E Ranch and found it harder and harder to go back to the ice-cold robot she'd hidden herself behind. She planned to get a thorough checkup at Doc's this afternoon, hoping he would be able to tell her why she was so easy to become annoyed over the littlest things.

Felicity rose to her feet, walked to the back door, and took up her favorite position on the swing seat. She curled up in the corner, leaving her right leg on the decking, and set the swing into a gentle rocking motion. Breathing in the clean, fresh country air was a soothing balm to her restless soul. She closed her eyes, listened to the animals and birds, trying to get her tight muscles to relax. She let her mind flit from one thing to another, not really concentrating on where it was taking her. She heard the sound of footsteps on the timber decking of the veranda from a distance as she rocked the swing. She slammed her foot down onto the decking and froze as she began to count. Shock reverberated throughout her system as the penny finally dropped. She opened her eyes to see Luke standing before her, concern for her on his face.

"Are you all right, honey? You look like you've seen a ghost," Luke asked, moving to her, squatting down in front of her, the palms of his hands rubbing her thighs.

"Yeah, I'm fine. What time is it?"

"Time we were heading out for your appointment with Doc. Are you sure you're all right?"

"Yep. Let's go. I can't wait to get these stitches out. They're driving me crazy."

"Okay. Come on," Luke stated, holding his hand out to help her up.

Moments later they were in Luke's SUV, heading to Doc's.

* * * *

Felicity was surprised she didn't have to wait in Doc's waiting room. She was called to go right in to his consultation room. Luke stayed out in the waiting room, giving her the privacy she had asked for, thank goodness. She knew he didn't like to leave her alone but had appeased her this time. It didn't take Doc long at all to remove her stitches, which was a relief. The scar below her knee was still a bright pink and unsightly, but Felicity didn't care. She was still alive, and that was all that mattered.

"All right, is there anything else I can do for today, young lady?"

"Um, yeah. Can you give me a pregnancy test?"

"Sure thing. If you would just go into the restroom over there, I need a urine sample to test."

"Thanks," Felicity replied, taking the specimen jar from Doc.

She was back a few minutes later and waited with bated breath for Doc to complete the test. Doc leaned back in his chair and looked at her expressionlessly. Felicity began to become agitated. Then a smile formed over his wrinkled face, his blue eyes sparkling as he looked at her. "Congratulations, Mama. You're pregnant."

"Oh my. Are you sure?" Felicity asked, her hand covering her mouth in shock and awe.

"One hundred percent sure. Now, I want you to take these prenatal vitamins every day, and you are to come back in one month's time for another checkup."

"Thanks, Doc," Felicity replied, hugging the elderly man, then left the room.

Felicity was quiet on the way home, not sure how to feel about her unplanned pregnancy. One minute she wanted to shout from the rooftops and let the world know, and the next she was scared how her men would react. Would they be happy or would they be angry? Not that it was all her fault. It did take at least two to tango. She was feeling rather unsure of herself. Doubts crept in, the worst-case scenarios filling her mind.

"Felicity, what's wrong?" Luke asked, giving her a quick glance, then looked back to the road.

"Nothing, I guess I'm just feeling like a have a case of cabin fever. I haven't been able to do much and it's making me crazy."

"Don't worry, hon, you'll be back to normal before you know it. How about going for a ride with me when we get back?"

"Hmm, as much as I would love to take a ride with you, what I'd really like to do is soak in the tub with a bit of oil to get the moisture back into my skin. I haven't had a bath for over a week. That big tub is just calling my name."

"Sounds perfect. Can I join you?" Luke asked, grinning lasciviously.

"Mmm, I think you all should join me. Do you think Tom and Billy will want to take a bath with us, too?" Felicity asked, hiding her grin.

"Well, what do you think, honey?"

"I think they'll probably be in the tub before I'm even undressed."

"I don't think, honey. I know," Luke replied with a chuckle.

Felicity couldn't contain her amusement any longer. She burst out laughing, knowing Luke would realize she'd been pulling his leg. He joined in her laughter, taking her hand in his as he drove her toward home.

Chapter Thirteen

Felicity had been soaking in the tub for at least ten minutes and wondered why she hadn't been inundated by her men yet. Luke had left her to go in search of Tom and Billy, but she had expected him to bring the others back to her by now. She exhaled loudly, the noise echoing throughout the large bathroom. She needed to be loved by her men, wanted, needed their hands and mouths caressing her body to the heights of arousal only they could give her. She laid her head back against the rim of the tub, thinking of the small life encased safely in her womb. She was so torn by her feelings. She was filled with joy and love one minute, thanking God for the miracle of the life growing in her body, then despondent, not knowing how her lovers would feel. She was going to have to find the backbone she had lived with for most of her life, tell her men she loved them, and then advise them they were going to be fathers. She couldn't go on not knowing how they felt about her, and she couldn't hold her feelings back any longer. She was sick and tired of hiding part of herself from the men she loved with her whole being.

Felicity sighed again then sat up to wash her body. By the time she was done, her men still hadn't appeared. She stepped out of the tub, dried herself off, wrapped the large towel around her body, and then removed the clip holding her hair on top of her head. She brushed her hair out until it crackled with static electricity and brushed her teeth. She took one last look in the mirror above the vanity and tried to hide the hurt she could see in her own eyes. She turned, heading to the closed door.

Felicity stopped in the doorway, her jaw dropping as she saw the bedroom and her men. There were scented candles flickering on every available surface in the room, vases of flowers, and flower petals strewn about. She let her eyes track the scattered petals, realizing they led to the bed where her three men lounged naked on the sheet. They all had damp hair and were totally, gloriously naked. Every single one of them was sporting an impressive hard-on that had her mouth watering. She watched as they each extended an arm in her direction, beckoning her to their sides.

Felicity held up a hand to stop them from speaking, but didn't move away from the open doorway. She was determined to say her peace before things got out of hand, knowing once they started on her the only sounds she would be able to make would be sounds of passion.

"I have a few things to say before we go any further. I'm pregnant and I love you all so much. I understand if you can't return my feelings and if you aren't ready to be fathers. I will leave and let you get on with your lives. I can't hold back anymore. It's too painful not being able to tell you how I feel, trying to keep my emotions buried. I've done that for most of my life. You three have awakened the living, feeling being I truly am, and I can't go back to that robotic person. I refuse to go back there." Felicity stood waiting for a reaction with bated breath, her arms crossed defensively over her chest, her eyes lowered to the floor in front of her.

Felicity felt and heard them move, and she raised her head, staring at them uncertainly as they moved toward her, the sight of their cocks bobbing with their movement fascinating the woman in her. Tom stopped inches from her, his bare toes touching hers. He lifted her face up to his and stood staring down into her eyes.

"I have loved you from the first moment I saw you. I couldn't survive without you by my side. I already knew you were pregnant, sweetheart. We've been loving you for over a month now, and not once did you say we couldn't have you. I have never not used a condom with a woman I've had sex with, until you. I couldn't stand the thought of anything coming between you and me. I was hoping you would become pregnant with our child. I wanted to have an excuse to hold on to you forever," Tom said emotively. He leaned down, placed a kiss on her mouth. The kiss was so full of love and emotion, she had tears coursing down her cheeks. She wrapped her arms around his neck and kissed him back. He slowly eased the kiss back, holding her by the upper arms to steady her. He moved away from her, allowing Luke to take his place.

"Honey, you are so beautiful, and I love you so much it hurts my heart and soul to leave you every time I go to work. I fell in love you the instant I saw you and had to convince these two boneheads to let me live here. I needed to be here near you, every day. You have filled my life with sunshine, my heart with love, and have made my soul complete. I am so full of love for you and our baby it hurts, but it would destroy me not to be with you," Luke whispered, his arms wrapped around her waist, holding her body against his. He moved back a step, leaned down, and kissed her with such love she felt her heart opening wide to accept the love her men were bestowing on her. Luke weaned his mouth from hers, gave her one last quick kiss, and then released her.

* * * *

Billy moved forward to take Luke's place. Felicity squeaked as he yanked the towel hiding her body from him, picked her up in his arms, and took her to the bed, placing her on the cool, clean sheet and following her down. He ravaged her mouth with his own, not holding anything back. He swept his hands up and down her body, touching her anywhere and everywhere he could. Their tongues dueled, teeth nipping, savaging each other with love and passion. He withdrew his mouth from hers, panting hard as he stared down into the deep violet blue of her eyes, a tear leaking out the corner of each eye as he held her tight beneath him.

"I love you, baby. I love you more than I can ever put into words or express with my body. Don't ever leave me. I would die without you. I love that our baby is nestled in your womb. To me, it's the proof of our love for you. I can't wait anymore, baby. I need to fuck you. Now," Billy stated through clenched teeth.

Billy moved his hand down to her cunt, testing her readiness for him. The pool of liquid cream he found dripping from her entrance had his cock throbbing hard. He sucked one of her nipples into his mouth, gently grazing the hard peak with his teeth before sucking on it hard. He groaned as their woman arched up into his mouth, demanding more from him. He didn't disappoint. He moved to her other breast, treating it to the same stimulation, then kissed and nibbled his way down her torso until he reached her mound. He kissed the top of her slit, flicking his tongue out, giving her clit a quick lick. He was surprised yet awed to hear Felicity cry out her release from one lick of his tongue. He moved down between her splayed thighs, wrapping his arms around her upper leg and spreading her more. He dove for her cunt, growling in the back of his throat as he tasted her cream. He couldn't get enough of her.

Billy removed one of his arms from around her thighs and shoved two fingers into her tight, wet channel, pumping them in and out of her body relentlessly. He licked and sucked on her clit, thrusting his fingers in a fast, furious pace. He made sure to glide over her sweet spot with every stroke, wanting to push her to the heights of ecstasy. He grunted as he felt the warning signs of her impending release, flicking his tongue over her sensitive nub faster, pumping his fingers deeper until she was sobbing out her pleasure. Her internal walls clamped down onto his buried digits as she screamed loud and long. He growled again as her milky white cum splashed out onto his chin, into his mouth, covering him, her, and the bed with her pussy juices. He kept his fingers and tongue working on her sex until the last spasm faded away. He felt his chest expand with his love for her and satisfaction he had never felt at bringing a woman to such an explosive climax. He sat up, moved his hard cock to align with her, and plunged in with one hard thrust.

"God, baby. You feel so good. I can't get enough of you, Flick. I can't get close enough to you. Come here, darlin'," Billy said as he sat up on the bed, pulling his woman up with him.

They both groaned as his dick inched in a bit deeper, her cunt clenching and releasing around his hard rod. He held her still as Luke moved up behind her and knew Luke was preparing their woman so she wouldn't be hurt from their double penetration.

* * * *

Felicity moaned as Luke began to massage his gel-coated fingers over her little puckered rosette. Even though she'd read about anal sex and ménages, she'd never even dreamed she would end up living out her fantasies. She sobbed out a breath as Luke pushed two fingers deep into her ass. She felt him stretching her as he pumped his fingers in and out of her tight back entrance. She turned her head, searching for Tom. She didn't have to look far. Tom was just moving up beside her, high up on his knees, his cock close to her mouth.

Felicity opened her mouth and swirled her tongue around Tom's cockhead. She licked and nibbled, paying close attention to the small slit in the top of his hard flesh. She loved the taste of her men's cum. They all tasted similar but also different, which she loved, as she was able to distinguish between them in the dark of night. She opened her mouth wide, drew her cheeks in, and sucked him down. She set up a slow, easy rhythm to begin with, breathing deeply through her nose then relaxing her throat muscles, and took him to the back of her throat. The sound of Tom's groans heightened her own pleasure and arousal.

Felicity stilled for a moment as Luke withdrew his fingers from her ass. Her pelvic floor muscles clenched and released, her ass begging to be filled again. She felt the blunt head of Luke's cock push into her body and moaned around Tom's dick. She pushed back onto Luke's rod, impaling herself until she felt his body against her ass and back. She sucked Tom back down her throat, getting back into a rhythm only she could feel as she pleasured her man.

Felicity hummed around Tom's cock as Luke slid his cock back to the tip. As he pushed back into her tight anus, Billy pulled his cock from her cunt then slammed back into her. The two men in her tight holes set up a fast, furious pace, pounding in and out of her body. She picked up her pace, bobbing up and down on Tom's cock, using her tongue to massage the large vein running the length of his flesh and the sensitive bundle of nerves beneath the head of his penis. She was on desire overload.

Felicity groaned as pleasure radiated out from her womb and cunt, down her legs, making her toes curl, and up her torso. She felt the warning, tingling warmth and knew she wasn't far from a massive orgasm. She didn't even realize she was keening in the back of her throat as she gave Tom fellatio. The walls of her pussy and ass rippled up and down the lengths of the two cocks pumping in and out of her holes. She felt her pelvic-floor muscles, as well as the rest of the muscles in her body, tightening in preparation to explode. Her legs shaking, her stomach trembling as her body rose to heights she'd never reached before. Tom yelled and shot his wad down the back of her throat, a hand fisted into her hair as he held her to him. She gulped frantically, making sure to swallow every drop of his cum. She withdrew her mouth from his penis, threw her head back as dark spots formed before her eyes, and screamed out her release. She felt her body clamp down hard on the two cocks in her cunt and ass then felt her body expunging her cum to drench herself and Billy. The orgasm went on and on, not letting up as her body shook with orgasmic bliss. She was vaguely aware of Luke and Billy roaring out loud as they held her tight to their bodies, pumping her holes full of their seed. Felicity slumped down on Billy and drifted away.

Chapter Fourteen

Felicity woke hours later to the smell of food. Her stomach growled, letting her know it was definitely time to fuel up. She quickly showered, dressed, and headed for the kitchen. She stopped in the doorway as she saw the men she loved and who loved her in return sitting alone at the dining table.

"Where is everyone?" Felicity asked curiously, moving into the room and taking a seat at the table.

"Well, they've all gone to town for dinner. I gave Nanette the night off and sent her home before you and Luke got back from Doc's," Tom said.

"Oh. Hey, the table looks nice. I've never seen candles on this table before. Oh, oh, who cooked?"

"Nan did, baby. She had everything ready before she left," Billy replied.

Luke and Tom got up and served the food. Nan had prepared a roast beef dinner with baked vegetables, greens, and carrots. Felicity inhaled the delectable aroma of the food as Luke put a plate in front of her place setting. As they consumed their meal, they all talked quietly about what needed to be done on the ranch. Felicity began to feel guilty. She'd hardly done any work since she'd arrived on the ranch and knew she should get back to work. She was about to broach the subject, but Billy placed a bowl of dessert in front of her, and since it had been a long time since she'd wanted to eat dessert, she decided to relish the last of her meal before talking to her men. Her men were watching her intently, making her think she had food stuck to the side of her mouth and face. She brought her napkin up to her mouth, wiped it, and glared at them as they smiled at her.

"What?"

"Nothing, honey. Finish your dessert," Luke said with a smile.

Felicity spooned up another mouthful and bit down onto something hard. She grimaced as she put her hand up to her mouth to remove whatever she'd found in her mouth. She looked down at the two fingers holding the object and felt her heart burst with joy. She felt tears prickling the back of her eyes then raised her head to look at her men. They were all staring at her with so much love, on their knees in front of her. The tears spilled down her cheeks.

"We love you, honey," Luke said as he took the ring from her fingers. He wiped it clean with a napkin then grasped her left hand with his.

"Love you so much, baby," Billy stated, taking her right hand in his.

"We love you more than we can say, sweetheart. We want to spend the rest of our lives with you, have babies, and grow old together. We've talked this through, and since I am the oldest of the three of us, we decided if you marry us, you would marry me on paper. You would still belong to Luke and Billy, too. We would all be your husbands in our hearts, no matter what that piece of paper says. Would you please do us the honor of marrying us? Spending the rest of your life with us?" Tom asked, sliding his hands up and down her thighs.

"Would I have to do man's work if I did?" Felicity asked facetiously, already knowing the answer.

"No," three deep voices answered immediately.

"We don't want you to work if you don't want to, sweetheart, but especially not while you're pregnant. We won't have you putting yourself or our child in any danger," Tom stated in a hard voice.

Felicity looked from one man to the other and let the love she felt for each of them shine from her eyes. She looked to Luke as he slid the beautiful, yellow-gold ring onto her finger. There was a large one-carat solitaire diamond with two smaller diamonds on either side. She had never seen such a perfect ring in her life. She launched herself from her chair down to the floor with her men. She wrapped her arms around them all, with a bit of difficulty since they were such big men, but she managed just fine.

"Yes, I'll marry you. I love you all so much. I can't bear the thought of living without you."

"You'll never have to, baby. Are you finished eating?" Billy asked with a crooked grin.

"Yes, I'm done."

"Good. Let's go fuck." Billy stated, scooping her up into his arms, practically running from the room.

Felicity giggled then glanced over Billy's shoulder to make sure her two other men were following. She smiled at them and then burst out laughing when they wiggled their eyebrows at her.

Life had never been so good.

THE END

WWW.BECCAVAN-EROTICROMANCE.COM

ABOUT THE AUTHOR

My name is Becca Van. I live in Australia with my wonderful hubby of many years, as well as my children, a pigeon pair, (a girl and a boy). I have always wanted to write and last year decided to do just that.

I didn't want to stay in the mainstream of a boring nine-to-five job, so I quit, fulfilling my passion for writing. I decided to utilize my time with something I knew I would enjoy and had always wanted to do. I submitted my first manuscript to Siren-BookStrand a couple of months ago, and much to my excited delight, I got a reply saying they would love to publish my story. I literally jump out of bed with excitement each day and can't wait for my laptop to power up so I can get to work.

Also by Becca Van

Ménage Everlasting: Slick Rock 1: *Slick Rock Cowboys*
Ménage Everlasting: Slick Rock 3: *Her Ex-Marines*
Ménage Everlasting: Slick Rock 4: *Leah's Irish Heroes*

For all other titles, please visit
www.bookstrand.com/becca-van

Siren Publishing, Inc.
www.SirenPublishing.com

CPSIA information can be obtained at www.ICGtesting.com
Printed in the USA
BVOW04s2352010415

394326BV00016B/93/P